"What is the meaning of 'whore?' "
Ruita asked in Tahitian, anger
rising in her voice.

I didn't hear an answer because
just then a hell of a fracas
broke out at the poolside. Ruita
and Kitty Merry were rolling on
the white sand, punching and clawing at each other. The actress'
halter was yanked off and Ruita's
blouse was ripped to shreds.

I ran over and pulled Ruita to her
feet, blood on her gorgeous face
from a deep scratch. Kitty had a
puffed eye and there was blood on
her over-red lips as she jumped up—
bare breasts moving like two enormous
pendulums—screaming words I hadn't
heard in years.

Much later, long after I had returned
to the boat, a Papeete cop arrived
looking for my Ruita. She had
disappeared. And Kitty Merry had
just been found murdered.

TWO HOT TO HANDLE

Murder in Paradise
The Coin of Adventure

Ed Lacy

Adams Media
New York London Toronto Sydney New Delhi

Aadamsmedia

Adams Media
An Imprint of Simon & Schuster, Inc.
57 Littlefield Street
Avon, Massachusetts 02322

For information about special discounts for bulk purchases, please contact Simon & Schuster Special Sales at 1-866-506-1949 or business@simonandschuster.com.

Manufactured in the United States of America

ISBN 978-1-4405-5798-9
ISBN 978-1-4405-3919-0 (ebook)

This work has been previously published in print format by:
Paperback Library, Inc., New York, NY.

"Murder in Paradise" and "The Coin of Adventure" appeared in a condensed form in Argosy Magazine.

Murder
In
Paradise

CHAPTER 1

We'd finished moving and cleaning our baskets of mussels and oysters——Ruita had a theory that a change in the feeding and water temperature might make for better pearls. We were about 20 feet down on the lee side of Numega, the protective mesh baskets suspended from anchored palm logs above us. As my wife worked over her prize baskets, golden-lip oysters imported from the Indian Ocean, I kept watching her creamy body, the wavy motion of her hair flowing in a soft black streak from the face mask, the easy movement of the strong hip and graceful legs, the good breasts and large brown nipples.

The sun, working through the blue Pacific, seemed to give a greenish dream-like aura to her golden brown body. Even the diving mask, the aqualungs strapped on her back, didn't spoil the nude beauty.

A school of *karava* fish, fantastically colored in the weird light, swam over to see what we were doing and added to the dream idea. I looked around carefully . . . they were merely curious, not being chased by anything bigger——like a shark.

Gliding down toward me, Ruita pointed below, then to a basket on my right which seemed to be coming apart. We covered the metal mesh with tar to stop the salt water from eating the wire, but somehow the tar had worn off——the bottom of this basket crumpled at my touch. One of the three giant mussels in the basket was already on the ocean bottom, being attacked by a great conch.

I swam down as Ruita put the other mussels in another cage. The conch already had its thick, ugly, snail body around the lips of the mussel and I used my knife to hack it

7

off. Ruita's breasts touched my back as she swam down beside me, pointed to where I'd damaged the mussel shell, then toward the surface. She took the mussel, kicked up toward the bright sun. We surfaced on our backs, shut the air valves, and using snorkles, backstroked toward the white beach of our island.

Unstrapping the lungs, Ruita pressed the water from her long hair, danced about in the warm sun until dry. "We were down for nearly 40 minutes, Ray. I'm starved."

I pulled her to me, roughly kissed the thick lips. Moving her lips against mine, she asked, "Your mouth is salty. Mine, too?"

"Aha. I go for your lips—salty or unsalted."

Her fingers playing with the hair on my chest, my wife poked at my worn swim trunks and whispered, "Then come, we will go home and eat, take our afternoon nap . . . although perhaps not in that order."

After rubbing each other down with a mixture of lanolin and coconut oils, Ruita slipped on a white blouse and blue Capri pants which went to her knees. The pants were from Papeete's swankest shop, the blouse she'd ordered direct from Paris. She stuck a couple of pale and sweet smelling *tiare* flowers in her hiar, then neatly opened the dying mussel with my knife . . . my eyes on the movement of her hips in the tight blue pants. She said, "This is one of the mussels we injected with pig-toe shell clam, from your United States, last year."

There was a small blister near the hinge of the upper shell, and in this soggy nest a sickly-looking white pearl the size of a pin head. "Hardly larger than the clam shell we put in," Ruita said. "But it was growing, in another four or five years, might have. . . ."

She felt of the slimy mussel body with her fingers, then tore the meat out. On the bottom shell was a flat, lumpy, pearl which shimmered a hundred dancing colors in the bright sunlight. I whispered, "A rainbow?"

Ruita nodded, gently holding it up on the palm of her hand. It was roughly about the size of a penny. "Ay, a large beauty of marvelous lustre. It must weight . . . at least 200 grains."

"What's it worth?" I asked, taking the cool hunk of pearl between my fingers, feeling the smooth skin.

8

Ruita shrugged. "You *popaa*—translate everything into dollars! Rainbow pearls are rare, but the rough, baroque shape spoils its commercial value. At a jeweler's shop it might bring a few hundred dollars. If it was perfectly round —$5,000. Look at the colors—perhaps someday I'll have this set in a pin. Come, I'm hungry."

She took both pearls and we started up the beach, Ruita running ahead like a kid, to chase the clumsy sand crabs— while I lumbered along with the damn heavy aqualungs.

Rounding a bend in the beach, Ruita practically ran into a tall man—a white man—although his skin was deeply tanned. Lean, well over six feet, with wide shoulders—he wore fancy flying boots, torn red walking shorts, plus a silly red beret atop brushed silver hair. He was finishing a wild banana and everything about him, from the cleanly shaved face to his walk, shouted a kind of nonchalant arrogance. Although his handsome face seemed vaguely familiar, I couldn't place him, wondered how the devil he'd got on *my* island.

Rushing toward Ruita, he took her in his arms, both hands cupping my wife's breasts. Ruita screamed as I dropped the skin-diving gear, ran pounding toward them. This big joker looked over Ruita's shoulder, calmly watching me as if he couldn't be so bothered.

Reaching the bend in the beach, I was tackled by two smaller guys. We all rolled in the sand. I tried to get my knees working, hit out wildly only to be expertly smothered in arms and legs. I found myself staring up at a slightly built man with very black thin hair and a long-ago-busted nose, sitting on my stomach, while a young Chinese fellow had a very firm armlock on my shoulders. They both wore expensive sport shirts and slacks. With a clipped British accent, broken-nose said, "Easy does it, old boy, we. . . ."

Ruita was kicking and scratching at the big clown who now held her at arms length, fingers still on her blouse. The tired-looking character using my stomach for a chair screamed at Ruita in French and English, "Love, don't bash his face! Not on his puss, darling!"

In this nightmare I was even more astonished to see Eddie, my old trading partner, suddenly come running towards us, yelling, "Matt, let go—that's Ruita!"

The tall goon under the crazy beret released my wife,

9

smoothly ducked one of her fists, stepped back to give her a mock bow. "Thousand and one apologies, Mrs. Judson." His deep booming voice projected so it actually seemed to hit with its power.

The two men holding me stood up. I shouted at Eddie, "What the hell is this?"

"Hello Ray," Eddie said, battered brown face a warm grin. "Hi, Ruita. Didn't you see our schooner come in? We're anchored in front of your house."

"We were . . . underwater," I mumbled, knowing the words sounded foolish. Brushing sand off, I got to my feet. The older man with the flattened nose wrinkled his sunburnt face with a tired smile.

"Sorry chap, but we had to ground you for your own protection. Matt's a bloody slugger, hits like the hammers of hell and. . . ."

I ran toward Ruita, the big guy watching me come with his bored, nonchalant air. I wasn't sure I could take him; he had a few inches in height on me, looked lean and muscular hard . . . but I was going to give it a try. The Chinese fellow came along side me as the big man boomed at Ruita, "I sincerely apologize and all that rot." A slight odor of rum hung on the words. "Really had no idea this ravishing beauty was your wife." This last was tossed at me, of course.

"You thought I was 'merely' an island girl you could have your fun with!" Ruita screamed, talking Tahitian—as she always did when angry.

The big man grinned at her—had this way of pressing his lips as if about to spit on the world—answered in perfect Tahitian, "You are quite wrong, beautiful one, I have my fun with *all* women. It is expected of me."

For a second Ruita stood there, mouth open, then asked in French, "Are you mad?"

"As to being mad, few people can truthfully answer yes or no," he said in fast French. "I am Matt Gregg, the male sex symbol, *the* screen personality, my dear." This loon yanked off his beret and struck a pose, showing Ruita a profile of his face. The oddly familiar puss was attractive in a kind of rugged way.

To my surprise, Ruita suddenly giggled up at him. I stopped at her side, aware the Chinese fellow was next to

10

me. Eddie said. "This *is* Matt Gregg—Ruita and Ray Judson." Eddie's thick fingers pointed at the other two men. "Walt Sing and Herb McCarthy."

We all nodded and Mr. Sing now took a step away from me. Matt held out a large hand and still feeling as if I was moving in a nightmare, I shook his mitt, mumbled. "Matt Gregg . . . ?"

He turned to the others, boomed, "Behold the puzzled expression on Mr. Judson's face! Obviously he has never heard of Matt Gregg, despite all the heavy dough we spend on publicity. Don't you ever go to the movies in Papeete, Ray?"

"The last time I was there they were playing a Hoot Gibson western over and over. . . ."

"Ah, yes, yes. I have seen your pictures in *Paris Match!*" Ruita cut in, talking English now and sounding like a dizzy movie fan. She even turned to smile at broken nose. "And you, you are the famous director."

Herb McCarthly clasped his hands over his head, like a pug. "Such is the empty bubble we call fame, a blooming whore, as a far wiser man has already called her." He nodded at the young Chinese guy. "Walt is Matt's secretary."

"A pleasure to meet you," Sing told us.

"Now in the. . . . What are you doing on Numega?" Ruita asked. It seemed to me she was actually pleased at having this collection of idiots around.

Eddie pulled a stinking cigar stub from his suntans, lit it as he said, "Matt and Herb are in Tahiti, set to make a picture about the life of Captain Wallis, how he discovered the island and . . ."

"Polynesians discovered Tahiti," Ruita cut in. "Captain Wallis was merely the first *popaa* to visit the island, although it is possible a Spaniard, Mendana, sailed by Tahiti in 1595, nearly 175 years before THE DOLPHIN anchored in Papeete."

"Eddie was quite right when he told us you have a vast knowledge of island history, Mrs. Judson," McCarthy said. "We are hunting for an island with mountains, similar to Tahiti, on which to shoot our picture."

"We're on Matt's schooner," Eddie put in. "Ray—wait

11

until you see it—a beauty of a ship." He sounded pleased about things, too.

The director waved his hands in the air. "Numega might prove an ideal location for. . . ."

"Since the picture is about Tahiti, why do you not make it there, or on Moorea?" Ruita asked, straightening the *tiare* blossoms in her hair, as if she didn't mind this invasion of *our* island . . . as if we were all making goddamn small talk!

The director pulled out a pack of filter cigarettes, passed them around. Nobody took any. He lit one, holding the cigarette in the crotch of his middle fingers. Everytime he raised the butt to his lips, to puff, his fingers made a V frame around his flattened nose. He'd been doing this for a long time—the space between his knuckles was deeply stained. "We can't shoot there because the president of our company can smell night life fifty miles away, and he's a bloke who loves to go on a toot, a hard drinking man! Actual picture making is not only ruddy work, but the delays send production costs orbiting."

"I'm the president," Matt added proudly—childishly.

Ruita asked, "Will you join us for lunch? We were on our way to the house."

"And we've come from your house," Matt boomed. "Comfortable and I love the furniture, but couldn't find your booze."

"Nice of you to look!" I snapped.

He showed me his perfect teeth in a practiced grin. "When I'm not working I stay stoned out of my mind. I was impressed—no locks on the doors; real South Seas hospitality. You two have it made."

"We were looking for you," Eddie added, as we started walking. Walt Sing handed the actor a new, and plain, corn-cob pipe full of tobacco and Matt walked alone and ahead of us. Ruita was bulling McCarthy about South Pacific history, while Eddie, Walt Sing, and I brought up the rear.

Sing told me, "You're a very lucky man, Mr. Judson, to live on an island of one's own with a beautiful wife—that's every man's dream, especially in this atomic age."

I nodded, still angry at this big jerk, Matt Gregg; remembering how he had touched my wife's bosom. Up close, Sing was far more compact than he looked, seemed all solid

12

muscle. No matter what he was doing or saying, he always kept his eyes on the actor. Watching Matt strut ahead of us was something to see; the cocky way he slouched along, the swing of his wide shoulders . . . a big punk challenging the world.

Passing the ancient copra shed, its roof a rusty mosaic of various flattened tin cans, I waved at Tupateka sitting in the shade as he puffed on a cigarette. He was a very old man who had the hut nearest our house. Happily sending out a cloud of smoke he waved both his hands at us, said in Tahitian, "Ah, Ray, I was on my way to tell you of the visitors. But now there is no need, you know them. They gave me a brand new cigarette—not have Cam-mels." He gently took the cigarette from between his heavy lips, held it up for me to see. "You hear before of Kent? Strange name, but good smoke. You try puff?"

I shook my head, thanked him for rushing to tell us about the visitors. Sarcasm is wasted on islanders—they're too honest.

Making another turn in the beach, we came in sight of our bungalow, and their boat, anchored a mile offshore, beyond the waves crashing and foaming on the red-brown coral reef. I'd expected one of these luxury yachts with a houseboat superstructure, the fancy windows and flashing chrome a rough sea would smash like a match box. But the clean white schooner riding the swells was a *boat;* sleek, trim, over 100 feet on the waterline, with the cabin not more than inches above the deck. On the beach, in front of our house, a neat inboard skiff was riding lazily with the breeze. The sight of the schooner almost made me forget my anger at Matt.

Eddie grunted, "Ray, wait 'till you go aboard! Diesels powerful as a liner, a dozen staterooms; the masts and booms are solid wood—not this hollow metal crap. Under sail she moves faster than a jet. . . ."

Ruita called back. "Ray, our guests are staying for lunch! I'm going to make them a true island meal." I was amazed at the gay note in her voice . . . suddenly wondered if she'd fallen for this crazy actor—told myself that was a real stupid thought.

Standing very tall, corncob stuck in his mouth at a jaunty

13

angle, Matt boomed, "Lovely Ruita, are you serious—nothing in the house but beer?"

"Good Australian export beer, and palm wine."

Tossing his pipe away he said, "I'll swim to the DOUBLE-TAKE, get us a bottle of rum." He started for the water but the director took his arm, suggested he take the skiff. Slowly, almost cat-like, Walt Sing moved toward Matt.

Eddie nudged me, whispered, "Watch this play."

"It's a long swim, well over two kilometers," Ruita said.

"Honey, I once swam to Catalina," Matt said, kicking off his boots, trying to push McCarthy away.

The director said, "Matt, cut it, there can be bloody sharks out there."

"Then give me a knife!"

I tossed my knife at his feet, said loudly, "The reef keeps out most sharks. Should be about two feet of water on the reef now but don't try standing out there—cut your feet, get coral poisoning."

Matt bent down to take the knife but McCarthy kicked it away. Drawing himself up to his full six-four, puffing out his chest like an idiot, Matt warned, "Herbie, out of my way before I lean on you! I want to swim, want the exercise."

The director stepped to one side as Walt Sing came on the run. The actor turned to face him, right fist cocked, let go a vicious punch, which the secretary slid under like a ballplayer using a hook slide. Sing's legs were tangled in the actor's and as Matt fell on top of the smaller man, he let go another terrific wallop which thundered into the sand. Walt was a Judo man; for a split second he and Matt seemed to be one, then he had a choke-hold on Matt's bull neck. The actor had one arm and leg free, thrashed about like a trapped animal; then as his face flushed he became quiet. Walt was pressing his wrist across the actor's throat.

Looking at me, Ruita screamed, "Stop them!"

I ran toward them, until Eddie grabbed my shoulder, damn near upending me . . . and winked.

The director, who'd been watching the two men from a safe distance, now said in a bored voice. "He's had it, Walt." Then he turned and blew a kiss at my wife. "Don't be alarmed, love, Walt is a kind of special tranquilizer,

14

necessary for a blooming giant like Matt. He'll sleep for awhile, soon be as good as new."

Crawling out from under the actor, Walt Sing brushed sand from Matt's lips, watched the heaving chest return to normal. Jumping to his feet, Walt brushed himself off, casually asked McCarthy, "Herb, shall I bring a bottle from the boat?"

The director relit his cigarette, fingers next to his busted nose, asked Ruita, "Would you care for spirits, or a bottle of bubble-water, my dear?"

"Palm wine will go with the meal."

"Fine, then let us get on with the food, I'm anxious to taste true South Pacific food. Walt and I insist upon helping you."

Ruita nodded toward Matt. "Shouldn't you carry him up to the house?"

"Nonsense, dear, Matt can take it. He's really rugged, could sleep on a blooming bed of nails and wake refreshed. Leave him be, he'll join us when ready."

Ruita glanced at me and Eddie said, "Matt's okay, let him be."

As we headed for the house I looked back at Matt lying there like a great fish thrown up on the beach; had this nightmare feeling real strong. I was sore at Ruita and Eddie. They seemed to be enjoying the unreality.

Ruita really became busy-busy in the kitchen, explaining to Walt and Herb how our kerosene refrigerator and deep freeze worked as she put them to slicing raw fish, squeezing limes. She changed to a plain blue *pareu* cloth wrapped around her good body, then raced out to climb a coconut palm, hunting for a type of nut which has a husk tasting like lettuce. Sing and McCarthy admired the way my wife's thighs hugged the palm trunk, probably making cracks about it.

When Eddie and I were away from the others, rinsing the flutter valves of the aqualungs with fresh water, I asked, "Where did you find this zoo?"

"Herbie's a boxing buff—wouldn't swap his busted beak for the Medal of Honor," Eddie said, lighting his stinking cigar again. "Soon as he saw my puss and tin ears in Papeete, became my boon buddy. Claims he's seen me fight in Honolulu and at the Hollywood Legion, years ago—

probably hot air. But they're paying me a hundred and fifty bucks a week for doing nothing but hanging out with 'em. How did you like the play on the beach?"

"That big bastard never meant to swim to his schooner."

"Might have, he's a wild flyer when loaded. But even if Matt wanted to, Herbie wouldn't let him risk his life—Matt Gregg is a ten million buck business. And don't let Matt's big talk fool you; when it comes to coin, both he and McCarthy are shrewd jokers. I hear they've sunk every penny they own into this picture, and expect to make a cool fifty million on the deal! Trouble with Matt, he never stops acting."

"Walt Sing is damn good. What's his job, Matt's keeper?"

Eddie nodded as he sponged the rubber tubing of the face masks. "Walt's another smart lad; graduated from some college in Los Angeles, he says. But, not too much of a talker. The deal goes down like this—Matt has to keep making like the big he-man, or as Herbie always says, keep the *image* going, be the action hero off and on the screen. Trouble is, Matt believes this hero stuff, at times. He's generally crocked, so whenever he steps out of line, any chance he might really get hurt, Walt stops him."

"If Matt ever connects with one of those wallops, he'll kill Sing. Wouldn't it be easier for Herbie to blackjack the he-man?"

Eddie laughed. "I offered to take charge of Matt—I can belt harder than he can, but you're not getting the image deal. Matt can't be walloped on the face, ruin his looks, the investment—and his gut is full of ulcers. In short; he can't be punched at all. So they play this game couple times a week—Gregg tries to kayo Walt before Sing puts him to sleep with this choke hold."

"Why did you bring the zoo here?"

Eddie slipped me a look of surprise. "Well, I haven't seen you and Ruita for over seven—eight months, and I thought you'd be interested in them using Numega for location."

"That's out! I don't want my island over-run with a bunch of nervous . . . !" Realizing I was shouting, I stopped talking, wondered what I was getting up steam about. Punching Eddie's thick shoulder, I said, "Good to see you. How's the HOOKER and the trading business?"

"The HOOKER stinks of copra, still has its crew of

16

roaches. Trading also stinks, as always. Market for copra is shot. The cutter needs a new set of sails, which is why I'm working for these clowns. Also, as usual, I'm hunting for a steady girl. As the movie crowd says, so what else is new?" Eddie burst out laughing, poked the stubble of whiskers on my chin gently.

I guess it was the sound of his real laughter, being with an old chum again. . . . I suddenly felt myself relax. What the hell, while our life on Numega wasn't dull, having a gang of lunatics around for a day could be an amusing change of pace. The truth is, the balance of the day and night passed in such hectic excitement, for our island life, I almost enjoyed it.

Matt soon came into the house, yawning, looking as if he'd just jumped out of bed. Ruita, still a beautiful bundle of activity, showed them how to catch the juicy, single-claw, coconut crabs. Tieing coconut husk with a long string, she expertly cast it over the crab holes in the sand; as Herb said, almost like trout casting. When the greedy crab stuck out his claw to grab the husk, Ruita jerked him high in the air, caught him behind his claw. Matt was good at it, but McCarthy was nipped. Walt Sing merely watched—mostly Matt.

Broiled with lime sauce, the crabs were added to the lunch Ruita knocked herself out to prepare. Matt was delighted, stuffing himself with big slices of papaya dipped in palm wine, coconut husk salad, plus a handful of vitamin pills Walt carried for him—as a chaser. As he loudly explained, "I have to watch my figure, part of my lousy profile. Liquor and food makes me bloated, so I gave up all foods but fruits . . . and I'll lean on the first guy who makes a crack!"

In typical island fashion, we ate so much we all went to sleep on the floor, to awake an hour later to jump into the skiff, race to the DOUBLE-TAKE . . . with a make-believe camera on her bow, where the chesty wooden statues of babes used to be in the old days. I was amazed they had no crew—Eddie said the regular crew was taking a vacation in Papeete. Both Matt and Herb boasted of their sailing ability, while it seemed the capable Mr. Sing knew enough about Diesels to pass as a ship's engineer.

The schooner was a beauty, with spotless cabins, a lounge

done in teakwood . . . everything shouting big money, but none of the garish 'yachting' crap to spoil her being a fine, seaworthy boat. While Matt played bartender, and they had the best stock of booze I've ever seen, the director ran off a sound film of the actor's last epic, a modern Western which I was just drunk enough to enjoy. Sing made a rousing supper of thick steaks and when it grew dark we took a couple bottles and headed for shore. Once inside the reef, Matt, Ruita, and I swam ashore; Matt wasn't lying; he was a powerful swimmer.

Ruita, still playing the big hostess, made torches of palm branches and showed them how to spear sleeping fish as we dashed about in knee deep water. She then built a fire on the beach and roasted the fish—without cleaning them—explaining to McCarthy and Sing the guts acted as a grease. Throwing the burnt fish into the sea, she yanked them out, pulled off the blackened skin, gave us the sweet cooked meat. Matt swore it was the best fish he'd ever had, and my wife went off into a lecture on this ancient Polynesian method of cooking fish.

While Eddie and I worked on a bottle of Scotch, the director and Ruita talked South Pacific history, and of course, he was amazed at Ruita's knowledge. He ended by making us an offer—we were to return to Tahiti with them; Ruita to read the script and act as a technical consultant. I, and I knew this was thrown in as an after-thought, was to help them find an island suitable for making the picture. For this, we were to be paid $3,000. Ruita was excited, but I told McCarthy we'd think it over.

As we all walked back to our house, I put my arm around my wife, whispered, "Hon, do you really want to get mixed up with these nuts?"

She giggled, "All you need with your breath is a dash of soda."

"Come on, I'm not that drunk—know what I'm saying."

Kissing me, she whispered, "Ray, they are loons, but as interesting as if they came from Mars. And we haven't been in Papeete for almost a year. Besides, I'd like to make sure they do an honest story of Tahiti—if I can."

When we reached the house Ruita started our hi-fi while Matt started pouring. Sailing on rum and Scotch, I went out to the veranda for the breeze. McCarthy came over, lit a cigarette. We sat on the steps as he said, "Ray, old chap, don't think we can use your island. Ruita tells me there are only a handful of natives and we'll need hundreds of extras. Be far too expensive transporting them here. Costing us a fat bundle as it is. . . . Do you know MGM spent twenty million remaking the BOUNTY in . . . ?"

I got angry again, he seemed to have forgotten I'd nixed the whole idea. In my crooked mind I had an idea they were all walking over me—even my wife. "Told you when you first mentioned it, no picture making on Numega!"

Herb slapped me on the back. "I know, but movie money talks big, so we learn to never take a NO. We might have offered . . . say . . . $15,000. for the use of your island. Would you still have refused, old chap?"

"Yeah! Money has no meaning here. We have over a hundred grand in New England banks—never bother to learn the names of the banks," I told him, over the smooth sound of jazz coming from the other room. All this wasn't quite true; we had the money, or rather Ruita had inherited it from her *mama-faa-amu,* which means the mother who feeds you, in Tahitian. Ruita's adopted missionary mama had not only left her the folding money, but sent her to college in Sydney. If Ruita never bothered with the money, I knew exactly what banks had the dough, kept a strict account of the interest . . . without really knowing why.

McCarthy rubbed his ugly nose. "Ray, I envy you, truly made life a piece of cake instead of a lousy rat race. Few blokes have the nerve and brains to take paradise in their hands when fortunate enough to find it. You and the lovely Ruita, perhaps the only really happy people left on this stupid bit of earth. Lord God, how I envy you!"

Herbie actually began to weep—drunken tears—and I was juiced enough to feel rather smug, and pleased. But even if I'd been cold sober, I probably couldn't have had any idea of the fool's paradise Ruita and I were about to enter.

19

CHAPTER 2

We dropped anchor in the horseshoe bay of Roogona, one of the smaller Marquesas Islands. The bay held the usual parts of a short reef . . . coral lumps and islets. There was a white sandy beach with its dock of rough coral blocks, a village of several dozen huts and the sun-bleached white church steeple . . . all at the foot of a mountain covered with lush green trees, salted with colorful patches of *frangipani* and *hibiscus* flowers. A few canoes were resting on the beach, while a large and ugly island schooner, flying the flag of Peru, of all places, was anchored several hundred yards from the DOUBLE-TAKE. It was a dirty boat, badly in need of paint.

We'd left Numega three days before. Ruita, now technical consultant for the picture, stayed behind to finish some work on our pearl breeding baskets, and to read the script. She had suggested we try the lonely Marquesas for a locale; pick her up on the trip back to Papeete.

I'd been badly hung over when I started the voyage and kind of dizzy ever since; didn't know exactly what I was supposed to be on this deal. Mostly I seemed to be a listening post. We all took turns at the wheel and at cooking. Matt, who remained fairly sober, and actually did a lot of exercises to keep in shape, bent my ear about what a great athlete he might have been if he hadn't become lost in the Hollywood rat-race. He blamed it all on his hair, which was a natural silver color, for some reason.

Walt Sing hated his job of being Matt's keeper, told me he wanted to make documentaries, especially about the lonely life and hard work of the Chinese laundryman in the States. Walt's father had sweated away his life washing, putting his son through college. Working for Matt and McCarthy was not only giving Walt some capital, but a chance to learn all the ins of movie production—when he wasn't choking the actor into submission.

Herb McCarthy was a cheerful cosmopolitan, who had lived and married all over the world. He told me, "I've learned you must have dreams, old chap, but more important, keep them in their blooming proper perspective, or they can ruin you. I'm aware I've turned out mediocre films, even if they are superior to the ruddy other dung being screened. But I've enjoyed myself, lived well, and when I start for that final horizon, I'll be able to truly say life doesn't owe me a damn thing. Oh, I still think I'll make a picture, some day, which will be a work of art, and believe me, Ray, film is a great art medium, no matter how badly it's been dirtied by morons and fast-buck bastards. I'll probably take that dream to my grave."

Of course, I listened politely to all of them; there wasn't much else to do. In a way I was content, the DOUBLE-TAKE was a tremendous ship, under full sail we made twenty knots. After the years I'd spent with Eddie on our HOOKER, it was a novelty to sail without copra stink or bugs. Matt and Herb were fair seamen and it was a boot for me to be sailing with Eddie again, his miracle navigation; by merely watching the water, the sea-weed floating by, the sound of the waves, the stars and the birds, he could sail a truer course than any captain working with full instruments.

Matt and McCarthy were pleased at the way Roogona looked, were anxious to go ashore. On the other schooner, its crew of islanders and several *popaas* were examining us through glasses, obviously amused at the sleek lines of our 'yacht.'

As we pointed the skiff toward shore, a small crowd of islanders, mostly elderly women in torn print dresses, were silently watching us. They were strangely quiet when we landed, seemed upset. A plump old woman in a tent-like worn grey dress was weeping loudly, the others trying to comfort her. Eddie, who spoke the island dialect, went over to ask where the French Administrator was; we'd need his okay to shoot the picture on the island. "Find out how many people are here," McCarthy called out.

21

There was this air of mourning about Roogona which spooked me, the Marquesas always effect me like this, as though the ghosts of the hundreds of thousands of islanders who died here of the *popaas'* TB and syph, were looking down, or up, at us.

Matt was busy smoking his usual new corncob, skimming pebbles for a few kids admiring his flying boots, when Eddie returned. "Little trouble here. That's Von Rumple's schooner out there, a tough Kraut thrown out of Samoa for smuggling. Lately he's been trading in the Tuamotu Atolls. Even though he was with the Foreign Legion in Indochina, he ain't exactly popular with French Oceania officials. In fact, the local government man is out on the schooner now. Von Rumple took a drunken young girl aboard. That's her grandmother carrying on. . . ."

The squat schooner was anchored some fifty yards from the coral dock we stood on and at that moment somebody was thrown off the boat, hitting the water with a sharp splash, to the laughter of the crew, especially a big blonde joker wearing a battered captain's hat, and little else.

A skinny old man with the wispy white beard of a goat came sputtering and thrashing to the surface, shook a tiny fist up at the schooner, shouting in French, then started swimming, awkwardly, toward the dock.

Kicking off his boots, hurling his pipe high in the air, Matt plunged into the blue Pacific, swam out to help the old guy. Eddie grunted, "Herbie, you wanted to meet the French Administrator, must be him out in the drink."

"That's the French Government here?" McCarthy asked, yanking out a tiny Minox camera, snapping Matt swimming ashore with the old man.

A shrill wail went up from the women, the fat grandma yelling, much as I could make of her dialect, "They have my Titin drunk! Of her own will I would not mind, but this . . . to force her while drunk is *hupe hupe!"*

I translated for McCarthy and Walt. "She says taking her granddaughter while under the influence of booze is a most ugly thing."

"By God, she's bloody well right, you know!" Herb said, busy snapping Matt placing this skeleton of a man on the dock, the wet and dirty linen suit making the old boy look pathetic. Spitting water, he drew himself up to his full five

22

feet, wrung out his beard, screaming in French at the schooner, "Be assured I shall report this in detail to the highest officials in Papeete! You swine shall be jailed!"

Matt said something to him in French, and as if seeing us for the first time, the old man tried to straighten out his wet suit, patched silk shirt, the long, snarled white hair, hanging to his shoulders . . . walked stiffly toward us. "You must pardon my appearance. I am Philippe Clichy, descendant of Napoleon's admiral. The troubles we island officials suffer! These beasts dropped anchor last night, to trade—although I run Roogona's only store, carry a large stock of goods. An hour ago they took Titin, a beautiful child of 13, aboard—first getting her so drunk on cough syrup she has no idea what is happening to her. Unhappily, our men are away making copra on an island some 63 miles north of Roogona, so I went aboard. . . . I'll make a complete report of this outrage, a. . . ."

"What's the population of Roogona, sir?" McCarthy cut in.

"309, at the last census," Clichy said as the old fat grandma let go another howl.

Flexing his thick muscles, Eddie said, "I think we'll pay a visit to the schooner."

The Frenchman turned to stare at Eddie, thin mouth open in shock.

Matt's booming voice split the air with, "We'll get the girl; let's go!" He actually sounded the hero, dramatically racing toward our skiff.

As we piled in after Matt, Clichy screamed at Eddie, *"A Lion Face! We want no lepers on Roogona!"*

This was Eddie's usual trouble on a new island; his flattened nose spread over the middle of his brown face, the puffed ridge of old scar tissue above his eyes, the cauliflower ears, did give him the look of a leper.

As Walt started the boat's motor, Eddie called back, "Don't be alarmed, Monsieur Clichy, my face is the result of absorbing leather, not germs."

Seconds later we were scrambling up the rough rope ladder of the schooner. The blonde giant, Von Rumple, two other ratty and beefy white men, plus a dozen or so crewmen of all sizes and shades of brown, watching us with amusement.

23

Up close, Von Rumple was a powerful bastard in his late 40's, several wounds and knife scars on his wide body. He wasn't armed, but one of the other *popaas,* a creep with a stringy black beard, some sort of foreign words tattooed on his heavy arms, held a belaying pin in his right hand, while the third *popaa,* a swarthy joker wearing red bedroom slippers and an evil sneer, had a knife stuck in the waist of his dirty trunks. If they had tried to knock us off as we came up the ladder, we wouldn't have stood a chance, but they were so damn sure of themselves, they let us come on deck. In broken, guttural English, Von Rumple asked, "Americans? This is a work ship, not a yacht, but welcome. . . ."

"Where's Titin?" Eddie asked.

Looking at us, talking over Eddie's head, Von Rumple asked, "Who is captain? I speak only to captain."

"I'm the captain, you'll talk to me!" Eddie grunted, rocking on his feet a little, the way he did when ready to brawl.

"We want the young lady. . . ." Matt began.

"Shut up!" Eddie snapped, rasping voice in sharp contrast to the actor's booming sounds. "This big bastard talks to *me!*"

Eddie fought as a middleweight years ago and even now didn't weigh much over 165 pounds. Von Rumple, who looked at least 220 pounds of solid man, screwed up his ugly, meaty face. "Watch what your brown mouth calls me! I see by your face you were a pug, and it means nothing to me. As captain, I order you off my ship at once, before I boot your ass off!"

McCarthy suddenly said something in German. The blonde giant smiled, clicked his bare feet like a damn fool, bowed, and answered in a flood of Kraut. Matt's hands were hanging loosely at his sides, his usual spitting-pout on his face. Walt Sing had moved in front of Matt, quietly watching the guys with the club and knife. I seemed to be the only one showing any nerves, I was shivering slightly. I was very much aware that Matt, Von Rumple, and I were the biggest jokers aboard; that I hadn't been in a real fight in years. The nightmare feeling swept over me—what was I doing on this strange boat, far away from Ruita and our island? Certainly be a hell of a stupid way of dying . . .

Touching his flat nose gingerly, Herb McCarthy told us,

24

"He says the gal is merely sleeping off a binge, nobody has got into her yet. . . ."

"Damnit, told you, let me do the talking!" Eddie cut in.

"Slow, old chap, slow," Herb said. "This can be settled without trouble."

"He lets Titin go—*now;* won't be any trouble!" Eddie said, never taking his eyes off Von Rumple.

"Just where is the young babe?" Matt boomed.

"Maybe I take pretty big fairy like you over *vahine,*" Von Rumple said, spitting at Matt's feet.

The action broke fast.

Titin, who had been sleeping it off on top of the cabin, staggered to her feet—a gorgeous girl in a dirty red and white *pareu* wrapped around an unbelievable lithe figure. Staring at us all with utter disbelief, she broke the silence with a childish giggle.

Eddie and Von Rumple both started toward her, Eddie popping the German with a fast left hook on his square kisser first. The Kraut did a kind of weird weak-kneed dance before hitting the deck. Eddie hadn't caught him flush—he wasn't cold—and I've seen Eddie "take out" bigger chumps than the German with his hook.

Sing went for the knife man, smoothly grabbing the hand holding the flashing knife above the wrist . . . seemingly pulling the man toward him, then, somehow, flinging the creep over his hips and against the cabin wall with a terrible crash.

Motioning for Titin to jump into his arms, Eddie then dumped her over the railing. I saw McCarthy neatly kick a rushing crew remember in the groin as Herbie jumped up on top of the cabin. I saw all this in the very small part of a split second; bearded bully-boy with the belaying pin had staked me out for himself. Feigning with my left, I jumped him as he swung, trying to get inside the arc of his club. I almost made it—the damn club grazed my left shoulder as I put all I had into a wild right wallop to his beard. It should have kayoed him, but he merely shook all over and started swinging the belaying pin again. I kicked his ankle, as an afterthought. He doubled over and Walt—passing by—without looking, gave him a Judo chop on the back of his neck, sending the guy tumbling face down on the deck.

Glancing around, I saw Eddie yelling at the crew in

25

Tahitian, telling them to keep out of it, not to be fools. When some heavyset cluck came at him, swinging like a gate, Eddie put an exclamation point to his few words by flooring the guy with a short right to the gut. McCarthy was kneeling atop the cabin, snapping pictures with his candid Minox. Titin was swimming gracefully toward the beach.

Von Rumple had staggered to his feet, glassy-eyed. Matt strode over to him, past Walt and myself, blocked a clumsy right from the groggy Kraut, set himself, clouted him with a terrific belt on the chin. Von Rumple was stiff before he crashed to the deck.

Dancing excitedly atop the cabin, Herb yelled, "Great, Matt, best pixs ever! Superb, absolutely superb!"

Eddie said, "Hell with pictures—let's get off here, fast!"

"Relax," Matt boomed, "I haven't even worked up a sweat."

With Walt at his side he took a few cocky steps toward the crew, asked, "Any of you stumblebums want to try me next?"

"Aw cut it," Eddie told him. "They don't know what the hell you're saying anyway."

"Walt, stand more to one side, out of the way," Herb called, the little camera covering one eye. "Hold your hands up, Matt."

With his fists raised like a boxer, Matt asked in Tahitian if anybody wanted to fight him . . . then, followed by Walt, he strode over to the railing, vaulted over—silver hair a technicolor flash—started swimming to the beach.

Eddie told McCarthy, "Come on, get off the cabin and stop all this slop! Get down to the boat. You follow him, Ray, then Walt!"

Walt picked up the knife which had fallen from the guy now laying at the foot of the cabin wall, blood streaming from his open mouth; hurled the cheese sticker into the Pacific as we scrambled down the rope ladder. Sing had the motor going and soon as Eddie was in the skiff we cut water for the beach.

The director sighed, "What I'd give for a blooming snap of Matt coming out of the water with that girl—Titin—in his arms! What an appropriate name—the child has a pair of headlights firm as those on a statue."

"Titin is Christine in Tahitian, as Ruita stands for
26

Louise," I mumbled, suddenly aware of the pain in my shoulder.

As if I didn't exist, Herb asked Walt, "You think they have the equipment in Papeete to radio a picture to the States?"

"Doubt it. Beside, those pictures generally print fuzzy," Sing said solemnly. "I suggest we wait until we return to Tahiti, fly the negatives and a story directly to the States. Meantime radio whoever is handling PR in Papeete to start thinking where to plant the story."

"You're right. I could develop this on the boat, but it's color film and I don't want to chance lousing it up," McCarthy said, as if discussing something important as atomic secrets.

Trying to rub the back of my left shoulder, I told them, "I've seen some candid camera loons, but you overdo it."

Herb smiled at me. "That snap of Matt carrying little Monsieur Clichy out of the water plus those on the schooner of him bashing the German bugger—worth a million bucks to us!"

I must have looked blank for the director touched his busted nose and added, as if talking to a backward kid, "The ruddy IMAGE, Ray! We're pitching Matt as the All-American male, every man and woman's dream of the dynamic, virile, freebooter. These pictures get it across better than a thousand bloody press releases. These are the *real* thing, Lord God!" He turned to Sing. "Walt, radio our seaplane at Papeete to drop over and pick up the film. . . . No, best I talk to the flacks myself on this; too big to handle indirectly. Should be able to leave here by tonight, dock in Papeete by the end of the week." McCarthy seemed to be talking to himself as Eddie shut the motor and the skiff glided up to rest its bow on the sand.

Titin and Matt were surrounded by the old women and McCarthy started snapping pictures again. With her wet *pareu* clinging to her, Titin, now fairly sober, revealed the curves of compact hips, wonderful breasts and tiny nipples; the clean, strong lines of her shoulders and good arms. Her face was standard cute, for any young girl, with the soft, black hair flowing down to the basketball behind. Skin a creamy gold, eyes the shape of lush almonds, long legs a little on the sturdy side.

Clichy had changed to a dry linen suit, as worn and sweat-stained as the other one, and an old straw hat. He was strutting about, shaking a World War 2 carbine at the trading schooner, mumbling in fast French.

Matt was accepting the gratitude of Titin's grandmother with practiced modesty; his whole body one casual stance, an arm around the girl, who barely reached his chest . . . his big fingers resting in their favorite position—cupping one of her firm breasts. Happy to be the center of attraction, Titin was trying to tell everybody about the fight, the heroes we all were. They must have gotten her crocked on hair tonic, not cough syrup, there was a horrible rose scented halo around her words.

The bell in the little church steeple began making a racket, while the old women buzzed about wanting to roast a pig for us. McCarthy got Matt aside for a whispered conversation, then they started talking to Clichy about using Roogona for their movie. But the old Frenchman kept shaking his head violently, waving his carbine and beard, shouting he could talk over nothing until the trading schooner left the harbor. As we piled back into our skiff, with him, and headed for the boat, I didn't see Von Rumple or the others aboard . . . wondered if they'd gone below for guns.

Circling the schooner, Clichy shouted through cupped hands he was ordering them to raise anchor and leave at once. After a moment the schooner's motor began to cough, then the anchor chain came rattling up. The schooner started a lazy circle of the harbor, heading for the opening.

I felt a wave of relief, mixed with the pain in my shoulder, until Eddie shouted, "The bastards are going to sideswipe the DOUBLE-TAKE!"

Grabbing the carbine from Clichy's claw-like hands, Matt told Eddie to head directly for the schooner. The actor shouted in French for them to change course, then taking careful aim, he splintered a spoke on the helm as we veered away from the schooner! The islander at the wheel spun it around quickly, forcing the big ship to heel for a second, then steered directly for the pass.

I was impressed. Considering the 100 or more feet separating us from the schooner, our speed and bouncing around in the schooner's wake—it was a hell of a shot.

28

Eddie blinked, asked, "Was that luck, or can you do it again?"

Matt fired a second time; splintered another spoke. We heard the helmsman yelling for more speed. Von Rumple appeared at the railing, waving his fist and cursing through puffed lips.

Matt wanted to shoot off the German's cap but Herb put his little camera down long enough to tell him it was too risky. When Walt took a step toward him, Matt handed the carbine back to Monsieur Clichy.

Returning to the beach, Eddie rubbed my shoulder with coconut oil, still talking about Matt's sharp shooting. Matt, Herb and Clichy were having a long talk, asking how soon the men of the island would return, the general weather, and a lot of other nonsense. We all went out to the DOUBLE-TAKE, along with Monsieur Clichy and a very old islander, who still had all his teeth—he was the only member of the Roogona Council around, the Chief and the others were making copra. I found a bottle of liniment to use on my shoulder, while Matt, Sing, and McCarthy now sported tiny blue glass viewers from black ribbons around their necks. We circled the island in the skiff—a good 50 miles in circumference—with the three of them busy pointing out "locations" through the blue glasses, which seemingly showed how it would all look in film. There was a great deal of technical talk . . . of which I couldn't care less about.

Reaching the village hours later, completely shaken by the pounding the powerful skiff had taken, it was agreed the movie company would return within 15 days. Each islander, kids included, was to receive an outright gift of five cans of beef and fruits, a carton of American cigarettes, and two bottles of aspirin. Whenever any of them worked before the cameras, they would be paid 500 Pacific Francs per day— about $5.75. The Chief, and each Roogona Council member, would also be given an electric clock. Monsieur Clichy was to be paid 5000 francs for any loss in trade the gifts caused his store, and a free stock of twist tobacco, cloth, and canned goods. The entire Roogona population would be on hand by the time we returned, and have cleared a strip of land near the village for Hollywood carpenters to erect an "authentic" Polynesian village.

Although Matt and McCarthy were now anxious to reach Papeete as fast as possible with Herb's rush-rush pictures, late in the afternoon we stopped to eat a pig Titin's grandmother had roasted in an oven of hot stones, taro and fruits. Herb McCarthy made a short speech in Tahitian, assuring the islanders the company would remain on Roogona for at least a month, and make everybody rich. Matt not only consumed an enormous amount of fruit, but delighted the islanders by walking a 100 yards on his hands. He also gave me a swift pain by confiding in me, "Crazy man, the Chief and the others wanting electric clocks—and no electricity on the island!"

"What's so odd about that? Owning such a clock, or an electric toaster, is a symbol of prosperity—like some of you movie characters who have swimming pools and can't swim."

"I swim like a fish and never owned a pool in my life," Matt said. I gave up arguing with him.

By nightfall we were headed for Numega, the DOUBLE-TAKE foaming through the Pacific like a speedboat, under every inch of canvas she could carry. I thought we were taking a hell of a chance, but Eddie merely gazed at the stars, sniffed the wind, announced there wasn't any danger of sudden squalls.

In the morning I was astonished to see Titin walk out of Matt's cabin, wide feet cramped into hideous, spike-heeled shoes, but not even a silly red evening gown or make-up spoiling her young beauty. The others didn't seem surprised at all and Titin said she'd always wanted to see Papeete. After a couple of painful hours, she kicked off her shoes, then changed to a *pareu,* spent all her time listening to jazz on the lounge stereo and drinking ginger-ale. Both Matt and Herb were very business-like now, didn't allow anybody to take on a load.

Eddie told me sadly, "How do you like my luck; with the scarcity of single girls in the islands, I have to have a goddamn movie star with me when I stumble across a Titin. My ugly puss can't compete with a profile."

Although they all paid polite attention to Titin, and Eddie tried hard to make time with her—showing off his muscle control as his muscles snaked up and down his shoulders and arms—during the little free time he had off from piloting—there was a new kind of tenseness on the voyage back to Numega. Everything centered around the snapshots Herb had taken. It was decided *Life* would be given the honor of displaying the "image in action" in the States, *Paris-Match,* the *London News,* and *Oggi,* in Europe. Matt said it was a darn shame Hemingway was dead—he would have been "the" man to write captions for the pictures, while both the director and Walt thought James Michener would be dandy—if they could get him.

Actually, I spent more time with Titin than the others. She kept asking me silly questions about life in Papeete, the price of clothes there. I found her as amusing and boring as all the "important" talk about the lousy snapshots. Despite all of Titin's obvious charms on display under her thin *pareau* . . . it probably will sound trite, but for me it was very true: after Ruita there weren't any women worth fooling with.

Keeping full sail on, with all of us sleeping only a few hours between watches, exactly 52 hours later we dropped anchor off Numega's old reef—which had faithfully protected the little island from traders and "civilization." The warm sight of Numega was like seeing an old friend. I went ashore with Eddie to pick up Ruita, McCarthy urging me to "make it snappy, Ray, we want to be on our way to Papeete within an hour." I wanted to tell him he could shove the whole deal, but was too excited at the thought of seeing my wife to start an argument.

As I was kissing and hugging Ruita, mentioned the rush the others were in to reach Papeete, she surprised me by saying she was anxious to discuss the script with McCarthy. Within minutes Ruita had tossed a few dresses into a bag, was ready to leave. Tupateka came around to ask if I had an extra pack of cigarettes, and without our mentioning it, it was understood he would keep an eye on our windows and boats—in case of a storm. Puffing on a "Cam-mel," he watched Ruita pack with a puzzled air, asked, "Why such hurry? The boat is outside the reef, no need to go with any tide?"

"The, eh . . . others, are in a great rush to reach Papeete," I said, rubbing my shoulder—the soreness was practically gone—and almost feeling like a stranger in my own house.

Tupateka nodded as though I'd made a profound state-

31

ment. "Ay, there is a great hurry to go there—and the return trip is always slower. You be gone long time?"

"A month or two, perhaps longer," Ruita told him, tucking the bulky movie script and some notes under her arm as I took the suitcase.

Tupateka mumbled, *"Aita peapea,"* meaning it didn't matter, and walked us down to the skiff as Ruita reminded him to look at our pearl buoys every other day.

Eddie was sleeping on the sand and I awoke him gently—he sometimes came awake swinging. Sitting up, stretching, he waved at Ruita—who was quite a picture in a red flared skirt, blue and white striped boat-neck blouse, and bare footed. Her jet black hair was piled atop her head a la a picture of Brigitte Bardot she'd seen in *Réalités*—except she had a tiny blue orchid over one ear.

Jumping to his feet, Eddie gave Ruita a friendly kiss, grunted, "Let's shove off." I wondered if the both of them were suffering from the movie itch, or worse yet—from ambition. I could remember many a day when it took Eddie hours to decide if he would arise to pee.

Once aboard, sails were raised and Ruita was introduced to Titin, who immediately lifted my wife's skirts high to admire the material. Then Ruita sat down with McCarthy and Matt, started telling them what she thought was wrong with the script.

Eddie and I took the wheel. I could hear Ruita saying, "Of course, you know in actual fact, Princess Purea was 45 years old and quite fat when she met Captain Samuel Wallis. Another thing; while it is true Tahitians had never seen iron, thought iron nails were some kind of fruit from a tree . . . even tried planting the nails . . . and it is also true that nails became such a favorite gift to the women that Wallis had to post armed guards—to stop his sailors from literally yanking out every nail on the DOLPHIN and sinking it . . . I object to the islanders being pictured as 'simple children.' You forget we Polynesians were bathing three and four times daily when the whole of Europe stank of dirt and sweat! Perfume was discovered to cover the body odors of the court ladies. Some place in the story it must be stressed that islanders were living a full and happy life when *popaas* were freezing their pale *derrières* in European caves, ignorant of fire; that our canoes were navigating the Pacific when your ancestors feared water, thought the stars evil eyes!"

"Honey," Matt boomed, "we're making a movie, not writing a history book. Might use this bit about Wallis firing on the Tahitians when they first flocked to greet him—thinking they were attacking him. You sure of that?"

"Of course. Europeans could only conceive of people rushing at them as an enemy—many islanders were killed, yet they were 'civilized' enough to forgive and forget," Ruita said.

"That's a nice bit, good dramatic possibilities—I'll think about it. But in the love department we'll have to keep Princess Purea a slim, young doll . . . fits in with the escapist image of the romantic island bimbo you know . . ." McCarthy's clipped voice said, as Ruita went off on a lecture about the hypocrisy of Western sex customs.

Yawning, Eddie asked me, "How's *your* image this afternoon, Ray?"

But that night was a true dream, Ruita and I in a comfortable cabin bunk—making love to the sweet clean tune of racing water hissing on the other side of the hull. Later, as we made sleepy small talk, she told me, "I seem to have lost that big baroque pearl we found in the giant mussel. The first time we saw Matt—when I was fighting with him—I must have dropped it. I've carefully examined the beach, but a wave could have carried it out . . ."

"*Aita peapea* . . . we'll grow others," I mumbled, my hand on warm curve of her belly. "Hey, what do you think of Titin?"

"A beautiful child."

"Crummy thing, Matt taking her to Papeete."

Ruita shrugged, many soft things moving, then kissing me she whispered, "You still hold on to your silly *popaa* morals. Titin came because she wanted to, would have reached Papeete sooner or later. She looks upon it as a kind of heaven, and nobody would be able to convince her otherwise. What's more, she told me Matt isn't much in bed, rates Herb, Walt, and Eddie as superior lovers."

Falling off into a deep sleep I mumbled, "Eddie? He never told me he was getting with that."

"Titin was quite puzzled at not being invited to this bunk," Ruita said, kissing me again.

33

A day later we closed in on that most beautiful of all sights—the approach to Tahiti. With Moorea behind us, we lowered sails and started the powerful Diesels soon as we saw the beacon atop Point Venus. Sailing through the pass, we stopped at the customs station on the tiny island of Motuiti, opposite the Papeete waterfront. And from the speedy attention the officials gave our *permit de séjour,* I realized what a big deal the movie company was in Papeete.

Almost with the ease of handling an outboard, Eddie backed the DOUBLE-TAKE to the quay, not far from where our old HOOKER was bobbing on the swell, and near a large, four engined ex-Navy flying boat.

I felt great. True, Papeete's ratty-carnival atmosphere, now combined with the hard sell of the new tourist hotels— tourists were water-skiing not far from us and McCarthy had radioed for two rented drive-it-yourself cars to be waiting for them . . . I knew all this would annoy me after a few days. But I looked forward to seeing the bustle of shops on the Quai de Commerce, an old friend like Mr. Olin's ritual of wine and rice cakes.

The movie company had a suite of rooms in the Grand Palm Hotel, a six story, elevator, affair built since I was last in Papeete—and for the next few hours Ruita and I were in a whirl of meeting new people—everybody so busy-busy.

Kitty Merry, the golden-haired, short, sexboat who was to play the princess in the epic, was pretty in a dull and hard-boiled way—the practiced leaning forward to show off her big breasts in the low cut blouse phoney as her name. There were several featured actors, the head cameraman, key grip, carpenters, make-up . . . Buddy, a queer and nervous young man—head completely shaved—who was "director of the second unit"—whatever that meant. He'd just returned in the seaplane from shooting "sky and cloud backgrounds." The public relations man was a very tense joker, looking young enough to be in high school instead of dashing around the rooms as if he had the itch. The only calm person seemed to be Molly Watson, the script woman. She was in her mid 50's, very pale, grey hair in a severe bun emphasizing the harsh lines of her thin face—yet I also realized she'd once been quite a beauty. The efficient type, Molly seemed the gal Friday of the outfit, and always working, quietly listening, taking daily Orinase pills—calmly telling Ruita she'd been a diabetic for years.

There seemed to be a thousand details to be straightened out and Herb McCarthy was in high gear. Kitty Merry started to fuss with Matt, coyly pouting he had been away from her arms far too long. Matt cut her act short with a fast kiss plus a solid slap on her backside, then went into a huddle with McCarthy and the publicity man, while waiting for *the* snapshots to be developed. All this nonsense was starting to drag, I suggested to Ruita we go to the quay and look at the old HOOKER, but she said she had to stay around to press for her "script changes." I noticed Kitty was studying Ruita, probably wondering where my wife bought her chic Riviera dress.

Eddie and I went down to the HOOKER, passing an excited Titin with Wal Sing—his arms full of packages—he'd taken Titin shopping at Marie Ah You's swank shop. I wanted to stop at Quinn's Tahitian Hut for a beer, but the place was full of loud tourists. Our cutter was a beautiful sight—like an old man still full of strength—even if it stunk of the stale odor of sour copra, and giant roaches greeted us on opening the cabin hatch. We had a couple of warm beers on deck, as Eddie decided he had much sleep to catch up on, before collecting his pay—seeing about the new suits of sails for the rugged cutter.

I wandered back to the hotel. The great snapshot deal had been finally settled—junior, the PR man, was taking them back to the States in the morning on a T.A.I. jet. Herb McCarthy proudly showed me the blown-up snaps, like stills from any of Matt's action movies. I was in the corner of one photo—looking a true ocean bum with my long hair, more than a stubble of whiskers. Herb said Ruita was busy with Molly Watson going over the script.

Although the Pacific was less than a two minute walk, the hotel had an idiotic swimming pool—in the shape of a palm leaf, of course. Matt was in swim trunks, stretched out on a beach mat—sipping a drink. Kitty was next to him in a skimpy bikini. Although very short without her high-heeled shoes, her compact figure didn't have a wrong curve—almost as if she'd been turned out on some factory belt line.

35

Kitty was angry—about something—while behind his sun glasses Matt seemed to be dozing. I decided to get a shave and haircut in the hotel barbershop. My deeply burned skin, dirty sport shirt, worn slacks, and torn sneakers caused a couple of plump tourists getting shaved to stare at me with pop-eyed uneasiness.

Gossip is Papeete's main amusement and no matter how crummy I looked, the barbers knew I was from Numega— I soon heard them whispering to the tourists I had an island of my own and was a "millionaire." The shop opened on the terrace overlooking the pool and the barber had finished shaving me, was starting to cut my hair, when I heard Kitty Merry shout, "What the hell you mean I can't look Polynesian? When make-up finishes with me I'll . . . !"

"You will look a Hollywood beauty made-up as an islander," Ruita cut in, talking slow, studied, English. "Please understand, this has nothing to do with your acting ability. But the fact remains your features are far too thin, as are your ankles. By Polynesian beauty standards you are not . . ."

"Matt, do I have to be insulted by this native whore! The hell with that crap about hunting for location—I know damn well why you were away so long—having your tomcat fun with this brown bitch, and now she thinks she'll get my role!"

"What is the meaning of 'bitch?'" Ruita asked in Tahitian, anger rising in her voice.

I didn't hear Matt's answer—was out of the chair and running at the sounds of screams. There was a hell of a tableau at the poolside; Ruita and Kitty rolling on the white sand, punching and clawing each other—the actress' halter was off while my wife's hair was undone, blouse ripped. Matt was sitting on his beach mattress, lips forming his famous sneer, as he made like Rodin's The Thinker —watching the women battle. The terrace and hotel windows were full of spectators.

I pulled Ruita to her feet as she was cursing in hysterical French and Tahitian, blood on her tan face from a scratch. Kitty Merry had a puffed eye and there was blood on her over-red lips as she jumped to her feet—bare breasts moving like two fat pendulums—screaming words I hadn't heard in years. I looked at Matt to hold her; had my

36

hands full with Ruita. When he didn't move, I pushed Kitty into the pool with my free hand, snarled at him, "Do your act, hero—maybe this will get your picture in the Brickhouse Monthly!"

Matt glanced up at me with his studied arrogance—as if I wasn't worth getting up to fight. When Kitty gurgled for help, he nonchalantly stuck his long leg over the pool for her to grab.

I walked Ruita to the ladies room, trying to calm her. When she came out minutes later, with her blouse pinned up, we pushed our way through the rubber-necking tourists in the lobby, hailed a taxi.

Once in our cabin aboard the DOUBLE-TAKE, Ruita changed into another dress while I took care of the scratch on her face. Ruita was quite cool as she explained she had been trying to tell Kitty why Titin should play the role of the Tahitian princess. Packing her things, I said, "We've had it. We'll move to a hotel, or aboard the HOOKER, until we can find a boat to carry us back to Numega."

"No, no, Ray. While I understand that stupid little blonde's ambitions. I also feel a responsibility to remain with the picture-fight to see they give a balanced portrait of the islands to the world and . . ."

"Honey, they have their lousy 'images' so fixed in their moron-minds, they won't change a comma! What's come over you?"

"Come over me? If you think I intend to run from that hardfaced little . . . bitch! . . ."

Ruita and I had our first real argument in years and when Herb McCarthy came aboard to apologize for the company, I shouted I'd be on the HOOKER—if she was interested—and walked off the schooner carrying Ruita's bag.

Eddie was still snoring as I put her suitcase in the cockpit. Shaking roaches off a mat, I stretched out atop the cabin, wondering how in the devil I'd allowed myself to be talked into leaving the peace of Numega.

About an hour or two later, I saw Ruita talking to McCarthy on the deck of the DOUBLE-TAKE, still carrying the goddamn picture script under her arm. Walking off the schooner, Ruita came over to the plank, bridging the stern of the cutter and land, asked if I wanted to take her to supper. I said I wasn't hungry. Ruita said she'd be at the Waikki, a Chinese restaurant we both enjoyed, and walked off.

Twilight comes on fast in the islands and when the sinking sun turned distant Moorea's jagged peaks fiery red, I went looking for my wife. She hadn't been at the Waikki I was told. I had a lonely meal and a few beers, started for the hotel—then turned abruptly in the darkness, returned to the HOOKER. Although still steamed, I knew I'd been a stubborn fool: the movie was important to Ruita—somehow—if a bore to me. Smoking one of Eddie's horrible cigars, listening to him snoring below, I sat in the cockpit waiting for Ruita's footsteps, knowing exactly how I'd kiss and hug her by way of apology.

Footsteps coming aboard awoke me. Two of Papeete's police officers stood on the deck of the HOOKER: one an islander, the other a Frenchman with a tough, pitted face. He asked, "Where is your wife, Monsieur Judson?"

"I . . . eh . . . don't know. Why?" I asked, coming awake fast, frantically wondering if Ruita had been hit by a car.

"We wish to question her."

I shook the sleep out of my mind. "Question Ruita? What the hell's this all about?"

"About the murder of the American actress, Mademoiselle Kitty Merry."

CHAPTER 3

As Eddie and I entered the *poste de police,* we walked into Matt and his nervous public relations kid—leaving the police station. Placing a hand on my shoulder the actor told me, "Ray, count on us to stand behind you and Ruita —money, lawyers, anything you. . . ."

38

"Do you know where Ruita is?"

"No, man. Herb last saw her when she left my boat to see you on the HOOKER. It's a mess, but don't let it throw you. We'll be waiting at the hotel—remember, anything we can do . . ."

"Yeah," I said blankly, having no time for Matt or his whole goddamn movie industry.

Eddie and I took seats before the detective inspector's desk—a tough and efficient-looking official fresh from Paris. Americans generally consider all policemen outside the States—with the exception of the Canadian Mounties —a bunch of fools. From experience I know differently: a cop's a cop the world over—a London bobby, a Paris *flic,* can be as club-happy as a New York or Chicago bull. What amazed me was the relaxed, almost casual air . . . the inspector sounded as if he was investigating a minor traffic accident.

He told us Kitty Merry had been found dead in her room at 8 P.M. when a maid went in to turn down her bed. Because of the black eye, Kitty had ordered supper sent to her room, shortly before 6 P.M. She had a habit of playing rock and roll records full blast and when the bell-hop knocked on her door with supper she hadn't heard his knock. He'd left the serving table with food outside the door, phoned her from the lobby. Kitty had drunk poisoned coconut milk and the medical examiner placed the time of her death at about 6:45 P.M. "So, we wish to question Madame Judson because it is known she had a violent quarrel with the deceased this afternoon, and because the poison was—juice of the *cerbera* tree."

"What the devil has that to do with my wife?"

The inspector gave me a scowl, or maybe it was only a tired smile. "Monsieur Judson, I understand you're upset, but please do not raise your voice to me. Murder is a rare crime in Tahiti, certainly not good for our new tourist trade or . . ."

"Listen to me, Inspector: the dead woman attacked my wife this afternoon, after first insulting her, but when I last saw Ruita—long before the time of the killing—she had forgotten all about the incident. The fact is, I wanted to return to our island at once, but Ruita insisted upon working with the picture company . . . I mean, she wasn't

39

angry about the fight with Kitty." I was frightened and confused, wasn't saying what I wanted to.

The inspector lit a *Gitanes,* offered us the pack. I shook my head but Eddie took a cigarette. The detective said, "This *cerbera* tree is only found in certain islands of the South Pacific, including Tahiti, and also in Madagascar. Its juice is milky in color—would be unnoticed in a coconut drink. Very few people know that in ancient island time, *cerbera* was a favorite method of murder. But I am told Madame Judson is an expert on Polynesian history. . . . Now, let us go over again the last time you saw your wife."

I answered his questions truthfully—actually had no idea of the exact time Ruita asked me if I wanted to have supper with her, but I insisted it was after 6:45 P.M. Puffing gently on his cigarette, the inspector said, "While I applaud your efforts to defend your wife, do not try to lie to me. Whether you spoke to Madame Judson at 6 P.M. or 7 P.M. means little, for according to your own words she spent only a few minutes with you—meaning it could have been after she killed Mademoiselle Merry, if she did kill her, or before. You are not giving your wife an alibi—it takes but minutes to walk from the quay to the hotel."

Eddie's questioning lasted a few seconds—he'd been pounding his tin ear from the moment we'd gone aboard the HOOKER. But he shouted, "I've known Ruita for years—she wouldn't kill anybody! I know . . ."

The detective held up a beefy hand. "At this moment all of us actually *know* very little. I am not unaware of Madame Judson's name—which has never been touched with the slightest gossip—a rare thing in the islands—which is also why I can not impress upon you both too strongly the need for her to come forward. Madame Judson, as of this moment, is not charged with murder, merely a suspect. It may well be she indeed has an alibi. Surely you both must realize the fact she's in hiding is almost an admission of guilt, so . . ."

"How do you know my wife's hiding?" I cut in. "Maybe she's being held . . . some place?"

"A possibility. Another: Madame Judson may also be dead."

I felt like I'd stopped a kick below the belt buckle. *"Dead?"*

The inspector held up a heavy hand again. "Merely a possibility—there's a killer loose, for it was a murder and not any accident. *Cerbera* is hardly something one keeps around the kitchen. You are free to leave now. I stress, if you have any idea where Madame Judson can be, or if you should see her . . . bring her to me."

I asked, "What about the others . . . Matt Gregg, Mc-Carthy?"

"All the cinema people can account for their movements. Also, they have no known motive for killing the deceased."

Leaving the police station, Eddie said he was hungry and when I snapped, we had no time to waste, Eddie said softly, "Stop twisting like an eel without its head, Ray. Let's have a beer and a sandwich, start thinking."

As he was eating, Eddie told me, "I heard this when I first started working for the picture company—Kitty Merry would never be voted the most popular gal on the set. Before she became Matt's gal, she'd kept Herb's bed warm, and Walt Sing hated her guts because she called him the Yellow Menace, Fu Manchu, and crap like that."

"Why didn't you say this back in the police station?"

"What's it prove? If Herbie or Walt wanted to kill Kitty they would have done it long ago—back in the States. And how would they know about this *cerbera* micky? I'm an islander and I never heard of the junk. We have to think of. . . ."

"We have to find Ruita! She might be headed for the country, out toward Taiarapu Peninsula, perhaps stole a bike or a car."

"Naw, the cops certainly have all those roads watched. More chance Ruita stole a canoe and headed for Moorea, or even back to Numega."

"She'd never make Numega in a canoe." The words gave me a headache as I mouthed them.

"You know Ruita, always so proud of the long voyages the old ones made in their canoes. What puzzles me, is why she's hiding at all. Get that mad look off your puss—I don't believe that slop she's being held, or dead, or she had anything to do with Kitty's death, but . . . ."

"Eddie, stop talking like these other idiots, of course Ruita didn't kill her! What's more—I don't give a fat damn

41

if she did—I'm only interested in finding my wife, getting her out of Papeete!"

Eddie belched as he finished his beer. "Translate that into common sense and it comes out—we have to find the killer, if we're going to do Ruita any good. The police might beat us to the killer, but in their book Ruita is the top suspect."

"We're not detectives, don't know how to solve a crime. All I want is to find Ruita—now!"

"I'll buy that, but still think we have to find the murderer before . . . Ray, we're forgetting Ruita's only been gone four or five hours—she can be sleeping in some relative's house: What 'family' has Ruita got in Papeete?"

"We haven't been here in such a long time . . . I can't remember if she ever mentioned any . . . here." Suddenly I felt better: islanders have relatives on every islet in the Pacific. The logical answer was—Ruita didn't even know of the killing; after our spat she'd gone off in a huff to spend the night in the house of some aunt. True, Ruita had never spent a night away without telling me—but neither had we ever had a real fight before.

I glanced at the wall clock—it was minutes to midnight. "Let's blow—Ruita may have returned to the HOOKER."

"The police are sure to be watching the cutter."

"We'll check, anyway. Sure, Ruita *must* be spending the night with friends, unaware of the mess. She'll show up in the morning . . . but in the meantime I want to have a showdown talk with Matt and Herb."

Crossing Boom Road to the quay, we found the HOOKER empty of people—Ruita or police. Eddie went over to the DOUBLE-TAKE, to have a look; the regular crew was aboard. Standing on the plank leading to the stern of the HOOKER, staring at the night, I almost was waiting for Ruita to call my name in a whisper. I told myself to cut acting like a fool: tomorrow when she left some cousin's house, heard the radio news, our troubles would really begin! In the morning I'd hire Papeete's best *avocat* —in case Ruita didn't have a decent alibi.

All the lights were on in the hotel room—offices of the movie company. Matt, Walt, McCarthy, the young PR man, and the billiard-ball-shaved-head Buddy, were

42

huddled around a table covered with large photos and papers. The air was business-business.

Matt waved and Herb motioned for us to take a seat. Buddy read from a note pad, ". . . tomorrow we leave, via plane and the schooner, for Roogona, with the rest of the studio crew to be flown directly from the States to the island by the end of the week. Molly has already cabled Rose Marino's agent about Rose replacing Kitty—that's been confirmed by a return cable . . . Good thing we never started any interior shots in our California studio—with Kitty. Being swarthy, Rose will look more the native gal type. I figure, within a week from tonight, we'll be set up for our first exterior take on Roogona." He turned to the PR man, drumming on the table with his fingers—looking more than ever like a teenage school kid. "When you plane out tomorrow, make certain to take a script for Miss Marino."

"Don't forget to bring a supply of Molly's pills back with you," Matt added.

Junior nodded his tense, crewcut head. "Okay, okay, but I'll be busier than a two-bit whore on a battleship, plastering these on every front page across the world . . ."

He proudly held up a large photo of Kitty sprawled on the rug of her room, face a frightening death mask . . . and even in death her robe was open—showing a cheesecake picture of her legs. Something about the face hit me wrong. But I didn't have time to think of that . . . Ruita suspected of murder and these bastards making with the business-as-usual pitch!

". . . *KITTY MERRY MURDERED! ISLAND BEAU-TY SUSPECTED.* Simple caption heads are the best. Mention Matt in the next line to . . . Oh, Mr. Judson, I've been looking for you. Do you have a photo of your wife?"

I went for him, swinging. With a bored movement Matt jumped up, pinned my arms behind my back. Eddie stepped toward us but Walt Sing slid in front of him, said softly, "Please, Eddie—don't."

Trying to shake Matt off my back, I had this terrible nightmare feeling again, heard myself shouting, "You greedy lice—smear your own mothers for a headline!"

"Mr. Judson," the PR man said, backing away from me, "we didn't invent the murder—it's a reality and we

43

have to ride with it. Certainly it can't be hushed, so our only course is to play it big. I assure you we're not happy about it—forces us to postpone the picture spread of Matt rescuing Titin from the. . . ."

"Ruita never killed Kitty!" I yelled. "Why don't you wait until the case is solved before hitting the headlines?"

"Because the news story won't wait. I'm aware of slander and libel, Ray—we're merely stating facts: your wife is the prime suspect."

"The facts are Kitty was probably knocked off by one of you! I'm told she was Herb's ex-girl, that Walt hated her, and God knows what other petty intrigues are involved!"

Matt asked, voice low, "Ray, if I let go of you, can we talk this over like friends, sensible men? Kitty's death was a shock to all of us. Will you listen, for a moment?"

"Okay." I wanted to wake up, turn to Ruita and tell her about the horrible dream I had.

"And don't start swinging, or I'll have to clip you," Matt added, letting my arms go. "We're in enough crap now, without fighting each other."

"He's right, you know," Herb McCarthy said, coming over to me, fingers making a V around his nose as he puffed on a cigarette. "Sit down. You too, Eddie. Nobody is out to bash anybody else, we're merely reacting to a sticky situation we face. Now, let me put you straight on a few bloody matters. It's no secret I spent time with Kitty in the hay—so did hundreds of other men. Sex was a kind of barter system with Kitty—a deal not limited to the picture industry, either. Titin used the same means to reach Papeete. No real emotions were involved, so I didn't kill Kitty, nor did Walt, or anybody in this room . . ."

"That's what you say!" I cut in.

"Ray, the island police are not blooming idiots, they've checked us out. As it happens at the time Kitty was killed, Walt, Matt, several other men . . . were taking pictures of Titin trying on lace undies they'd bought her. They were all together from five to well after 7 P.M. As for myself, after Ruita left the DOUBLE-TAKE, I remained aboard with the crew, working out cabin arrangements for the company, when we sail tomorrow."

There was a moment of heavy silence in the room, like

44

the quiet of doom. Picking up one of the pictures of the dead woman, I stared at her bruised face, the hard, unseeing eyes, the almost sullen mouth. Something about her face. . . .

Walt Sing handed Matt a new corncob as he told me, "I admit I had no liking for Kitty, but if I killed every cluck making cracks about my being Chinese—the death toll would be in the thousands. For what it's worth, Ray, I don't believe Ruita did it."

McCarthy passed Matt a tobacco pouch as the actor boomed at me: "Ray, both you and Ruita are still on our payroll and we stand by our people. I know—may sound like a snow pitch, but I mean it. We'll pay for the best lawyers from Paris, hire private eyes from the States . . . work out something. Perhaps it can be called self-defense. I'll testify in any court of the world as to Kitty's violent temper. In its own way, a movie company has influence that. . . ."

"With the Papeete police!" I wanted to add, but didn't. I suddenly felt terribly weary, knew I was wasting time with them—they all believed Ruita had killed.

Without listening, I heard Buddy ask Eddie if the HOOKER would be ready to sail in the morning. Eddie said, "You crazy? We're not sailing until this is straightened."

"I was going to load equipment on your ship, but . . . you come along whenever you're ready. HOOKER is too slow—we're ferrying most of our stuff via the seaplane, anyway. Always be somebody here at the hotel in daily radio contact with Roogona, so whenever. . . ."

I stood up, headed for the door, Eddie following me. Matt called out, "You have like half a haircut, Ray. I'm good with a scissors, let me finish the job."

Papeete was dark and quiet in the early morning hours —except for a few speeding cars. A truck full of singing men and women passed us, the Tahitian songs against the sad wail of a guitar sounding not unlike shrill hillbilly folk songs.

The bugs and sour stink of the HOOKER'S cabin were too much for me; I curled on the deck with a mat and blanket. The DOUBLE-TAKE was lit by work lights as supplies were being loaded. Wrapping the blanket around me tightly against the *hupi,* the cool night breeze sweeping down from the mountain, I dozed off to an uneasy sleep—only to snap awake moments later: I knew what it was about the picture of Kitty which seemed out of wack—her face was far *too* bruised and scratched! I could only recall Ruita blacking one eye, a few scratches on her neck.

I sat up, looking at the many stars—watching a jet passing far overhead in another world—listening to the rustle of palm leaves, the sound of crates being taken aboard Matt's schooner. My excitement turned to ice. Actually I wasn't certain how Kitty had looked when I was busy pulling Ruita off her. Also, a bruise might not show until a brace of hours later. My head ached from thinking in hopeless circles. Twisting in the blanket, I told myself to stop worrying—get some sleep, be ready to protect Ruita when she returned in the morning.

Coming out of the cabin, Eddie handed me the heel of a rum bottle. "Drink up, Ray. I can't sleep either. If I hadn't brought them to Numega, you and Ruita wouldn't be in this mess."

"Stop it. We're not Titin—knew what we were getting into. We both came because we wanted a change . . . I guess."

"Maybe. Well, get some shut-eye." Eddie relieved himself over the side, went down to his bunk.

The rum was so hot and harsh it wiped everything from my tired mind. The next thing I knew the roar of the seaplane taxiing down the harbor awoke me. Blinking at the early sun, I watched the DOUBLE-TAKE moving out—had a stupid flash thought: was Ruita in Matt's cabin?

The wake of the plane and schooner violently rocked the HOOKER. I dived over the side, for my morning toilet, then took out the old tin drum Eddie used for a stove, put on coffee. I even heard myself humming—have a big breakfast waiting for my wife, coffee strong as lye—the way she liked it.

By 10 A.M. I was ready to explode. Eddie came on deck, rubbing his head, yawning and breaking wind. He said, "Now we know where we stand—have to solve this murder ourselves. We. . . ."

"Eddie and Ray, couple of super dicks who couldn't find water in the middle of the Pacific! I let that movie

46

crowd fast talk us with their alibi bunk—big deal, all handing each other an alibi! Now they're at sea . . . Hell, how dumb can we get!"

"Running ourselves down won't get us any place," Eddie said calmly. "Ray, we're overlooking Papeete's favorite sport—gossiping. I think we should nosy about, pick up all the talk we can, sift the grain from the slop. People we know will tell us what they wouldn't tell the police. For one thing—we'll learn where Ruita is."

I nodded, afraid to say aloud what I was thinking: if my wife was alive she would have heard about Kitty's death by now, rushed to the HOOKER. "It can't do any harm, I guess. I'll go buggy if I don't do something."

Pouring himself a cup of coffee, Eddie said, "Not impossible Ruita's still asleep in some cousin's house, been up late shooting the breeze—long-time-no-see stuff."

Leaving the HOOKER, we decided we would return to the cutter every two hours. I was going to the police station, a few of the bars, while Eddie would take the rest of the joints. Ducking the frantic bikes and motorscooters, I reached the *poste de police* with my guts doing a rumba. The inspector told me Ruita hadn't been found . . . and a flood of relief swept my dizzy head: at least her body hadn't been found either. "Monsieur Judson, again I urge you to make every effort to have your wife come forward. Things grow worse for her with each minute she remains in hiding. Remember that."

I said I'd remember, and leaving the police station wandered around Papeete like a stranger. It had been so long since I'd last been here, I couldn't think of anybody I could talk to. I went in and out of bars, too tense to get high, racking my tired brains trying to recall any names Ruita might have mentioned knowing in Papeete.

Finally I returned to the HOOKER. Eddie was sitting on the cabin, chewing on a new cigar. Before he could ask, I shook my head. He shrugged his thick shoulders. "Nobody knows a thing about Ruita, which is good—bad news would travel. I dropped in to see Olin. Seems Matt, the great image, was swindled yesterday—bought a rainbow pearl for $16,000. The . . ."

"How big a pearl?"

"Olin mentioned it in passing—didn't say the exact

47

weight—but for that dough it must be a hell of a big one. Olin's kind of steamed at the movie people for not buying supplies from him, so he's happy Matt was suckered into buying this dud. He said Walt. . . ."

"Was the pearl a baroque—irregular in shape?" I asked, motioning for Eddie to follow me as I ran back to the quay.

"I don't know. What's so important about this pearl?"

"I'm not sure, but it could be the can-opener to everything!" I panted as we rushed by the many swank shops on the Quai du Commerce, finally turned into a narrow side street lined with Chinese stores, women wearing long slit gowns. As always, when I turned this corner, I had the feeling of stepping into another country and century—even if the street was a big tourist deal now.

Mr. Olin's office was the same rambling, two-story, wooden building which seemed ready to collapse, although he was one of the richest traders and money-lenders in the islands. The polite clerk told us to wait—but when I insisted we had to see Mr. Olin at once—he pressed a button of the intercom atop the battered counter made of old packing crates, spoke soft Chinese. Seconds later Eddie and I were rushing up the rickety stairs to the office.

Sitting behind his polished ebony desk, Mr. Olin looked his usual fat self—blue slacks ready to burst around his tremendous belly, silk shirt an outrageous red. The round face was still smooth as a flat pebble, but the silky tuft of hair like a tiny hat on his polished head was turning dull-grey. Holding out a pudgy hand, his shrewd eyes amused, he said, "Ah, Ray, it is good to see you. We shall have rice cakes and wine for . . ."

"I'm in a small rush, Mr. Olin," I told him, shaking his hand. "This rainbow pearl Matt Gregg bought—do you know if it was a baroque?"

"Even a fool would not pay thousands for a deformed pearl. I've seen the gem—of brilliant lustre and about 800 grains in weight. A beautiful gem of perfect shape. Why are you so interested?"

"I'm not—now." I didn't hide the disappointment in my voice. I had expected it to be the lumpy pearl Ruita had lost on the Numega beach, figured McCarthy or Sing had found it, sold it to Matt. "If it's a real rainbow, and so

48

large . . . why did you tell Eddie you thought Matt was swindled?"

Olin grinned, reminding me of those old cigar ads about the smiling man in the moon. "Ray, as an amateur pearl breeder you know there is no more difference between a cultured pearl and the so-called 'real' pearls, then between a baby born of natural sex and one born of artificial insemination—both are *real* babies. A person is a fool to spend such money for a single pearl when there is the possibility that any day the market can be flooded with large cultured gems. I did use the word swindle, because the tall actor is under the impression he bought a bargain, that the pearl is worth $50,000 on the open market. You know Henri Karl?"

I shook my head. Eddie said, "Isn't he one of the Belgians who came here from the Congo?"

Olin nodded, all his chins dancing. "He plans to use the money to open a bowling alley." Olin sighed, took a tiny brown hula doll from a cheap cardboard box on his desk. We all watched the hideous doll wiggle its rubber hips. "An era is ending. No longer is my stock of trade goods composed of smell soap, canned sweets, strong hair tonics . . . now I must carry this nonsense for the tourist trade. Karl is what they call a 'hustler,' a disagreeable type new to the islands."

"Was Bully Hayes, any of the old traders, any better?" Eddie asked.

"One knew he was dealing with brawn. A crafty brain can be far more dangerous, cruel to the point of . . ."

I wasn't in the mood for any of Mr. Olin's philosophical lectures. "Where can I find this joker?" I cut in.

"Ask at the Grand Lotus Cafe. Your friends, the movie people are big fools—bringing their supplies from the States. It would have been cheaper to buy from me. One of them, Walter Sing, a most educated young man, visited me. He wished me to back him in the building of a studio here, to produce pictures for this TV. I explained I only invest in things I can hold in my hands, store in my. . . ."

"Excuse me, Mr. Olin, but I have to go. If you should hear anything at all, concerning my Ruita, let me know."

"Certainly, my friend."

49

Starting down the trembling steps, I turned. "What's this Henri Karl look like?"

"Stocky, about 45 years in age. A fast man with a knife, it is rumored. However, he has an old knife scar running from one ear down to his neck, so perhaps he isn't so fast."

The Grand Lotus was one of the new buildings quickly thrown up for the expected tourist rush: a purple monstrosity shaped like a drum, with a roof of thatched pandanus leaves. It was on the airport road and, as Eddie and I paid off the taxi driver, a jet of the Transports Aeriens Intercontinentaux came in for a landing, screeching like a frightened bird.

The interior of the cafe had a large bar in the shape of a lotus blossom, dance floor, a door behind the bandstand leading to an office. Chairs were stacked on the tables and the joint was empty except for a bartender—a thin little Frenchman, the biggest part of him being his ratty puss—washing shot glasses. When I asked for Karl, the bartender said in loud French, "Monsieur Henri Karl is not here."

Eddie and I ran out of the cafe in time to see a big man, with a ragged pink scar disappearing from his right ear along a bull neck into a yellow Italian knit shirt. Heavy through the shoulders and hips, he didn't look fat. He was racing for an old Ford roadster parked in the shade of towering palm trees to one side of the cafe.

Karl got a tough break—he had to cross the front of the cafe to reach the clump of palms, so was only a few yards ahead of us, running heavily. As I sprinted after him, pounding like a truck horse, Eddie picked up a thick branch and threw it at Karl's legs. The stick hit the back of one knee and sent him sprawling, but the Belgian bounced to his feet like an acrobat as I reached him. He seemed to be fixing the waist of his dirty linen pants— and a flashing 6 inch slim knife appeared in his right mitt. In very good French he said, "Stay where you are! It was a legitimate sale, so tell your big actor not to send any goons after me!"

"Nobody sent us. I . . . ."

"I have seen him of the Lion's Face with them—you both work for the movie company!" He spoke coldly, eyes never leaving our feet.

"Listen, we're here on our own," I said. "Merely want to ask you. . . ."

"You—I've heard: your *vahine* is wanted for the actress' murder." Karl pointed the knife my way.

"Perhaps you can help my wife by answering. . . ."

"If you're not from the actor, I certainly have no reason to talk with you. Leave me alone—this knife is no stranger to human meat!"

Eddie picked up two rocks. "A knife is no better than the length of your arm, and that ain't no throwing cheese sticker. Why don't you first listen to what we want to ask instead of blowing your nose so much?"

"Bastards, I warn you for the last. . . ."

Eddie sent a rock whizzing by the Belgian's head. It missed by inches but hit the roadster behind Karl with a crash of windshield glass. Karl reacted normally—turned his head for a moment to see the damage—we both came in on him. Diving for his feet I saw a sickening silver flash before my eyes as he slashed at my face. There was the small thud of Eddie's fist landing. I hit the ground with a double thud—the first was me, the second being the stiff 200 odd pounds of the Belgian crashing on top of me.

Crawling from under him, fighting to get my breath back, I stood up. The bartender didn't come out, in fact it was very quiet until Karl coughed and then spit out a glob of blood. He sat up, trying hard to get things in focus with his glassy eyes. Feeling of his heavy chin, he muttered in French, "You have broken my jaw!"

"Naw, you'd be screaming with the pain instead of talking," Eddie said calmly, juggling the knife on the palm of his right hand. "Maybe the next time I'll bust it. Might even show you a couple of knife tricks, too."

"I haven't the money, every franc is tied up in my bowling . . ."

I said, "We don't want your dough, just some information about the rainbow pearl."

"It's all legal, I bought the pearl a year ago in Bali for 100 pounds, Sterling. I've been waiting for a rich tourist buyer—if the man is a sucker, it's still legal; not my fault if Monsieur Gregg thinks the gem is worth $50,000. Not illegal; perhaps in Los Angeles, or Paris, a pearl that size —who can say for certain what it will bring?"

51

"How did he know you had the pearl for sale?" Eddie asked.

"When the actor first came to Papeete I showed it to him, asked $20,000, but he wasn't interested." Karl touched his lips with one hand, stared at the blood on his fingers. He started to get up but Eddie snarled. "We can hear you better sitting! Ray, don't stand too near his legs."

"What's all this about the pearl to do with you?" Karl asked me.

"I don't know. You telling us Gregg wasn't interested when you first showed him the pearl, but yesterday, after he returned to Papeete, you offered it to him again and he . . . ?"

"No, he came to find me. Seemed angry and . . ."

"What time was this?"

Karl shrugged. "The exact time I can not say, but it was in the afternoon. He makes a firm offer, $16,000—American—take it or leave it. Well, I accept, fast. We get in my car and ride and he picks a jewelry store—has me stop. Chinese store. The actor shows him the gem, asks if it's real. That is all, not even what the jeweler thought it was worth. The Chinese say it's real, the biggest rainbow pearl he ever see. Monsieur Gregg slips him some francs, then gives me the cash—all in $100 bills. I make for Banque de l'Indochine, show them a few of the bills—make sure it is not 'queer' money. Then I sew up my bowling alley deal. That's all."

"Did he say why he suddenly wanted the pearl?" I asked.

"No. Nor was it my place to ask—or care."

"What did you mean—Matt, Monsieur Gregg, seemed angry?" Eddie asked.

"That is how he seemed. Not angry at me, but in a . . . bad . . . mood."

I tried to think, finally asked. "What shape was the pearl?"

"Perfectly round, of course." Karl laughed, sending out a bloody spray. "Even an actor would not pay such money for a badly shaped pearl."

I told him thanks. Eddie tossed the knife into bushes a good 25 feet away. As we started to walk, Eddie called over his shoulder, "Relax—and sit there . . . awhile."

"If this all you ask, why we make fight?" the Belgian asked, switching to broken English.

"You pulled the knife," I said.

"Who pays for the windshield?"

Eddie grinned. "Come on, what's a windshield to a bowling alley owner?"

Wiping his mouth with the side of one arm, Karl laughed again, called after us in French, "I want no hard feelings when I open my bowling alley, so I tell you one thing— means nothing to me. While he's looking at the pearl, Monsieur Gregg say in American, like talking to himself—but his voice so deep I hear him say, 'This ought to hold her.' That is everything I know."

Walking slowly back toward the center of town, Eddie chewed on a cigar, asked, "Think Kitty was 'her?' "

"Matt, the lover, was giving some girl a pearl he thought was worth fifty grand, so it wasn't for any one night stand. Even if he was buying it for a babe back in Hollywood, why the sudden rush? Why didn't he wait until the picture was finished, was about to return to the States? Or was this Karl lying about Matt saying, 'This ought to hold her?' "

"Naw, he was so glad to be getting off with only a fat lip, I think he was handing us straight goods. What would he gain by snowing us?"

"There's only two girls Matt would give gifts to here— Titin and Kitty. I can't see him giving Titin anything of real value."

Eddie grunted, "Leaves Kitty. But since she was his babe, and a gal who traveled on her back, Matt isn't gifting Kitty to get her into bed. . . . All starting to add up—oddly: Matt's away from Kitty about a week, hardly sees her, then rushed out to buy what he thinks is a $50,000 pearl. Why, that's. . . . !"

"Blackmail," I cut in.

"If the pearl wasn't found on Kitty's body, or in her room—then we got us a new reason for the killing— robbery."

"And it proves Ruita's innocence—she would not only know the true value of the pearl, but doesn't need gems nor money!" A glow of excitement warmed my guts, only to become a clammy lump. "But where is Ruita?" I asked myself, as we passed the market place. "I don't give a hoot who did Kitty in, only want to find my wife!"

"Me too, but there has to be a connection between the killing and what's happened to Ruita. I think we ought to go on Roogona: nobody is ever killed in Papeete except by a car, or too much booze. The movie people are the new touch, so our answer's, with them, not here or. . . ."

"Ruita must be in Papeete!"

"For all we know she can be a prisoner on the DOUBLE-TAKE. Even if she is in Papeete, and we find her, Ruita's still under the police hammer—we still have to bag the killer to free her. If she's here, the worst can happen to her is she'll be jailed. If she's in hiding, with her credit and friends, she'll be okay. Sooner or later, if she's here, Olin will hear, tell her where we've gone—to Roogona."

It gave me a chill the way Eddie was carefully circling in words what we were both thinking—*if she was still alive.* "I can't leave—I'd go nuts! What if she's hurt and me a ten day sail away?"

"Ray, stop it—if she was hurt or in trouble here, word of it would have reached us long ago. Another thing, they have a 30 day shooting schedule—then head for the States to finish the picture in a studio. Once they've gone, we're really sunk." Eddie stopped. I looked up; we were in front of the *poste de police.* "First let's see if we *can* leave here."

The inspector was very off-the-wall with us. When I said we wanted to sail the HOOKER to the Marquesas Islands, finish our job with the movie company, he told us, "You may leave Tahiti whenever you wish. When your wife is found, I will contact you via the motion picture office radio. I can tell you that Madame Judson is not headed for Numega—we sent a Navy plane out this morning; it would take a sailing vessel at least three days to reach your island, a sailing canoe much longer—no ships of any kind were to be seen heading for Numega. For the last time, I urge you, if you know where Madame Judson is hiding to. . . ."

"If I knew where she was, I wouldn't be standing here!" I snapped.

"*Atira!*" he growled, surprising me by saying, "Shut up!" in Tahitian, adding in French, "I warned you before not to raise your voice in here!"

"Sorry. By the by, if it isn't an official secret, was any-

54

thing of value found on the dead woman, or in her room?"

"Except for an extensive wardrobe, she had no valuables, only some costume jewelry, kept a little cash in the hotel safe. Why do you ask?"

"Everybody overlooks plain robbery as a motive for the killing. A thief . . ."

"I have not overlooked that, but crime is rare among the islanders. True, we have many *popaas* in Tahiti, some of whom have far from clean records. If death had been caused by a knife or a gun, it would seem possible the deceased surprised a sneak thief in her room. But, considering the method of her death, that is highly illogical."

I shrugged and as we started to leave, he asked. "When do you expect to depart Papeete?"

I looked at Eddie. He said, "Soon as we can——this afternoon."

We parted outside the police station Eddie leaving to stock the HOOKER. I went to Olin's. The old man was out but I left a note explaining we were going to Roogona, would return in a few weeks. I stopped at the picture company's hotel office where some young fellow with a game leg—and the usual tense face—told me he would send down several cases of liquor. "Your boat's far too slow to carry anything else."

"Send them at once, we're sailing in a few hours."

"Will do. We have obtained permission from Miss Merry's kin to have her buried in the islands. Soon as shooting is finished, we fly her body to Roogona to be buried high on the mountain, overlooking what would have been the scene of her greatest triumph, a fitting . . ."

"I know, and with a 66 flash gun salute!" I said, leaving.

Eddie's new sails weren't ready, but the old ones would do. Within a few hours we were headed for the customs station on Motuiti, anxious to clear the pass before twilight. I never could get more than four knots from our old motor and we had to go slower to avoid the tourists busy water-skiing. Near Motuiti Island, a kid in an outrigger canoe cut across our bow, forcing Eddie to come about. He was a strapping brown boy of about ten, shoulders already solid with muscle. He waved his paddle at us and feeling sure he must have a message from Ruita, I shut the motor. Coming

55

along side, he held up a long yellow fish, asked in Tahitian if we wanted to buy it.

I cursed him, and with an astonished look on his face, he slapped his elbow—an obscene gesture, shouted furiously, "Why you yell at me? You bad sonofabitch!" Then he threw the fish at us. It fell in the cockpit as I turned on the gas cock. Eddie tossed him a few coins, but the kid indignantly threw them back at us, paddled on.

While our papers were being checked at Motuiti, the detective inspector suddenly appeared, a hammy smile on his hard face. He and an island customs man spent an hour going through the HOOKER, even lifting the bilge boards —although anybody hiding there would certainly be asphxiated.

Finally, looking angry and frustrated, he returned to the office, told us to leave.

It was growing dark as we ran up sails, put on running lights, and hit a choppy sea. I took the tiller while Eddie opened the battered oil drum, lit the one burner gasoline stove resting on the bottom, started making coffee.

With a deep feeling of gloom, I watched the lights of Tahiti fading behind us. Among the creaking noises of our boom, the hiss of the hull slicing water, I heard a faint, *"Ray!"*

Jumping up, I glanced around wildly in the dim light, asked Eddie, "You hear that?"

Looking up from the 'galley,' he asked, "Hear what?"

"I heard Ruita calling me!"

"Come on, take a few drinks, get some rest. I'll take the . . ."

" Ray! Eddie . . . . . Ray!"

The voice came from the port side and I brought the HOOKER around abruptly as we both searched the railing. I saw her tan hand and a moment later pulled my Ruita aboard, looking like a golden goddess. Except for a snorkel and face mask, she was buck naked and trembling with the cold.

CHAPTER 4

Bundled in one of Eddie's old sweatshirts, strong legs wrapped in a blanket, Ruita sipped coffee as she said, ". . . That night, I suddenly realized we were really fighting over—nothing. I returned to the HOOKER to again ask you to have supper with me. However, foolish pride—fortunately—made me wait in a cluster of trees: I would surprise you when you awoke, came looking for me. But when the police came, I overheard them saying I was wanted for questioning about the murder . . . full of panic, I fled. You see, earlier, when I left you after our fight, I'd merely walked around Papeete, avoiding the crowded streets, couldn't prove where I was at the time of Kitty's death. So I hid."

"Where?" I asked, rubbing her cold legs, so happy I wanted to cover her with kisses.

"It was very simple. I have a cousin in Papeete, a man named Fumer, whom I haven't seen in at least 15 years—he was a sailor and away from the islands for a long time. I selected him of all my relatives in the city because he lives near the King Pomare Memorial, on the outskirts. Naturally they were delighted to see me and . . ."

"Didn't they hear on the radio about the police looking for you?" Eddie asked.

Ruita laughed—a lovely sound. "You forget, at one time I was an avid reader of French mystery novels. In order not to worry them with the police, and to protect us all, I didn't say I am Ruita, by my cousin—and their's—Nitu—who lives in Forliga, one of the Tuamotu atolls. It was a harmless deception, we are of the same age, and I was certain they hadn't seen her in years. Well, I knew I had to leave Papeete and that I would leave on the HOOKER. I had one of their sons buy me a snorkel and face mask—told them I was having an affair with Eddie and playing a joke on him—to make sure he wasn't sailing with any other girl. Naturally, they were interested in such romantic intrigues—several times a day one of their kids bicycled to the quay—and this afternoon raced home to tell me you were making ready to sail. He was the lad in the canoe. The rest was too easy—in the twilight as he paddled near the HOOKER, I put on the snorkel, went over the side of the canoe. When you stopped to bawl him out, I was hanging to your dinghy, under it all the time the police searched the boat at customs. Once we were at sea . . . here I am."

Eddie, who was at the tiller, nodded in admiration. "Ay, you have a beautiful head, inside and out, Ruita. Even if your cousins brag, they will talk about this Nitu—no word of your leaving Tahiti can possibly reach the police."

Playing with her stubby toes, I said, "Hell with Roogona now—we will head toward Easter Island, some place off the beaten track. With the cutter we can sail around the remote islands for months without. . . ."

"You want us to run, Ray?" Ruita asked.

"Run like hell! Honey, it was a mistake leaving Numega in the first place. I almost went crazy at the thought of you in jail . . . and the case against you is strong."

"But now that we know about the pearl . . . ?" Eddie began.

"Balls, we don't actually *know* anything, merely have us a new theory about the murder. I'm not going to chance Ruita being picked up—ever!"

Ruita asked, "What pearl?"

When I told her what he'd learned from Karl, my wife said, excitement riding her voice, "Whoever stole the pearl, believes it's worth a fortune—a perfect motive!"

"Ruita, I don't give a fat damn about the pearl or finding the killer! Can't you understand, we're in a mess and all I want is out!"

"Being on the run for the rest of our lives, Ray, isn't any 'out,' " she said softly, squeezing my hand. "Nor is it possible—planes, the radio, have shrunk the Pacific. With all the publicity, the police will never forget this case—sooner or later we'll be found."

"She's right," Eddie added. "If we don't show up in Roogona, they'll send out an alarm for the HOOKER. We'll be spotted, a plane sent for us—no matter what hunk of coral we're hiding on."

"Listen to me, we find some islet on one of the remote atolls, you put us ashore—we'll get along. In time you can return to Papeete and have Olin secretly cash a check, buy us plenty of stores—return months later."

"Ray, if Eddie returns to Papeete—no matter when— the police will grill him," Ruita said.

"Then we'll scuttle the HOOKER once we find our deserted island!"

"If you want to play it like that, I'll sink the cutter," Eddie said, without enthusiasm. "She's really half your's and . . ."

"Let's stop all this wild thinking," Ruita cut in, her voice gentle. "We've done no wrong, why live the rest of our lives in hiding? Eddie loves the HOOKER and we love Numega, our house, have our pearl hobby, our . . ."

"Both of you are talking with paper heads! We're not only dealing with the police—who are damn well convinced you murdered Kitty—but also with a very real killer! Honey, know what was driving me off my rocker back in Papeete, when I couldn't find you? I kept thinking you were dead! Another thing, we're involved with a powerful and ruthless movie company who'll stop at nothing to make more headlines!"

"Ray, Ray, take it easy, we don't have to make a decision this second, or this night," Ruita said, pouring a cup of the strong coffee. "From what you've told me, Matt and Herb, Walt, they all seem almost as upset as you were, about my being under suspicion. They did offer to help in any way they could. Let's combine both our ideas."

"What's that mean?" I asked, putting sugar in her coffee, stirring it with my finger.

"Well, as Eddie said, we have to go to Roogona, or the police will be sure I'm aboard, start an air hunt for the HOOKER. Once we arrive in Roogona, I'll leave the HOOKER underwater, using the snorkel again—hide on an islet, if there is one, or in the mountains. Be quite simple —remember, to the movie *popaas* all 'natives' look alike. Wearing my hair differently, I could probably be one of the extras and not be noticed! Also, I've never been on Roogona, to the islanders I can pass myself off as Eddie's girl."

"That's too much of a risk!" I told her.

"To go rushing off, on the run, would be more of a risk, dear. We reach Roogona, and as your slang goes, play it from there by ear. We can all work on the stolen pearl angle."

"Work? We're not detectives!" I shouted.

Ruita reached over to kiss me. "Ray, would I do anything to spoil our happiness? Be realistic, darling, even if we could find some empty island where living conditions are tolerable . . . how long would it be, a month, a year, before the inter-island gossip grapevine mentions a tall *popaa* and an island woman alone on some coral hunk, bring the Papeete police? We're safer going on to Roogona, where I remain in hiding, and see what we can learn about the pearl. If we learn nothing, find no clues to the killer, then we can always try your plan."

"But we're getting involved again! Why take *any* chances, let's get away while we can."

"Ray, Ray, we're involved in this whether we want to be or not," Ruita said. "We don't exactly have a free choice."

Eddie said, "She's right. If we're caught on the run— say, a year from now, what chance will we have then of finding the murderer?"

"Goddamnit, you both sound like kids playing at cops and robbers!" I snapped, and immediately was sorry I'd opened my big yap: Eddie and Ruita glanced my way, their brown faces telling me to stop acting the all-wise, big white *popaa*.

Eddie said, "Since the killer doesn't know we're on to the pearl, that gives us an edge. One thing is for sure, we have to go on to Roogona, or the cops will suspect Ruita being with us. Ray, you agree to that?"

I nodded—although I didn't agree.

"Okay, once there we'll see how the cards fall. Meantime, we have at least nine days to make plans, so no sense knocking our brains out now. I have a lime pie, anybody hungry?"

"I'm starved—a lime pie!" my wife said, eagerly.

60

As usual, when a Polynesian dismisses something from their mind, they really drop it: it minutes Eddie and Ruita were eating the pie, enjoying themselves. I guess if more people could do that, there would be less need for psychiatrists in the rest of the world.

During the ten days it took us to reach Roogona, Eddie and Ruita acted as if they hadn't care one—it was like the old days on the HOOKER. There weren't any fixed watches, whoever was awake relieved whoever was at the tiller, or did the cooking. Eddie was full of his old yarns about his days as a pork and beaner pug.

I was the only one full of worry. Twice we passed ships —a tourist liner so high out of the water it looked frightening; the other boat an old island tramp schooner. Each time Ruita remained below. But we had a hot argument when a jet streaked overhead and she stayed on deck, telling me, "Don't be silly, they're flying at 15 or 20 thousand feet, can't possibly identify me."

We slept and ate well, played cards and made small talk —as if this was merely another trading trip. All the time I was tighter than a drum in the rain, only relaxed when Ruita's demanding body was next to mine on the cabin bunk, in such a tight embrace even the HOOKER'S brazen roaches couldn't come between us. But after such passion sessions, I only worried all the more at the possibility of losing my sexy wife.

On the morning of the ninth day out of Tahiti, Eddie— with his usual instrumentless-but-on-the-nose-navigation— pointed to some ugly frigate birds wheeling above us, said we'd see the Marquesas before night. In the afternoon he nodded at a bright spot on the pale blue horizon, announced, "The reflection from Roogona's harbor."

Within another few hours we began to close in on the island, seeing the mountain top and later even the coconut palms. Eddie put the cutter on a new tack, bringing us on the rear of Roogona as twilight fell. Then we started a slow circle of the island, with me at the tiller and Eddie sitting on the bowsprit—a form of masthead piloting—listening to the sounds of the waves, able to tell if we were approaching water too shallow for the HOOKER'S modest draft. With our running lights off, we slipped into the harbor and ran along a hunk of shelf reef—a good mile from the main curve of the harbor and the village. Mostly the reef was under seven or eight feet of water, but here and there ragged bits of coral split the surface and there was this bit of coral —an islet—about 30 feet in diameter with a cluster of coconut palms and a few ragged bushes.

Ruita, sitting in the cabin hatchway, thought it would be an ideal hiding place. We dropped anchor some 50 yards away and I swam ashore. The little island was deserted, although from the few cans I stumbled over in the darkness, it was probably used now and then for a picnic grounds, or as a lovers' nest. I couldn't find a spring; and the rustling of coconut crabs in the night was a lonely and spooky sound.

Swimming back to the HOOKER I told them what I'd found and Ruita said, "It sounds fine."

"I'm not sure if there's water, but we'll be anchored nearby, so. . . ."

"No, you must anchor in the harbor. If the cutter is so far from the village, people will get curious. I'll take water ashore with me now," my wife said.

"She's right," Eddie said. "We anchor here, islanders and the movie crowd are sure to come out and visit the HOOKER. We'll row you ashore now with water and food."

"There are coconuts, I will not need other food. Nor will I make a fire."

I said, "Honey, wait up—you'll need food, a tent, a small gas stove."

She shook her pretty head. "Food will attract birds, while any fire might be seen. I shall need nothing but a knife, and not even that, really, for I shall live as my ancestors did— make a lean-to with palm leaves, eat well on coconuts and crabs. Ray, no argument, it will be simple enough for me to do—and safer. Believe me." She reached up and stroked my face.

I didn't go for the idea of her being there alone. Ruita must have read my thoughts, for she added, "During the day you musn't visit me, either, under any circumstances. But each night, at about this time, I'll swim to the HOOKER."

"That I don't buy—there can be sharks around. No, every night, when it's dark, I'll tell everybody I'm going fishing, row over. Eddie, do you have a pistol?"

"A Luger."

"Wrap it in oilskins. Ruita will take that, too."

"Ray, there's no need," she began. "I'll be perfectly . . ."

"Honey, I'll feel better if you have a gun. Otherwise—no dice."

"All right, but only to make you feel better."

Wrapping a knife and the Luger in a plastic cookie bag, Ruita tied them around her waist, along with a *pareu* cloth, Then taking off the sweat shirt and pants she was wearing, she slipped over the side of the HOOKER. Towing a can of water, she swam with a quiet breast-stroke . . . in order not to make waves, leave a phosphorescence wake in the dark water.

In the night, I couldn't see if she reached the islet. Eddie, who was leaning far over the side, listening, suddenly stood up, announced, "Ruita's on the island."

"How can we be sure? She might have had a cramp. . . . ?"

Eddie cupped his big mitts, whistled once. Seconds later there was an answering whistle. Grinning at me, he said, "Now stop worrying, put on the running lights while I haul anchor. If anybody asks why we stopped—we went aground on the reef in the darkness."

Using the motor, minutes later we dropped anchor near the DOUBLE-TAKE. The yacht was dark and quiet, only her riding lights on, while on Roogona kerosene lamps flicked dimly in some village huts.

Some distance away from the village—the spot the islanders were to clear for the movie people—a large generator began to purr and seconds later a great spotlight flashed, showing a marvelous street of stately huts, while on the beach near the set I thought there was a wrecked ship . . . but using glasses we saw it was a sort of sawed-off stern of an old English sailing vessel resting on the sand. Several white men in over-alls began hammering away on one of the larger huts.

Eddie said, "Guess that's how Papeete looked two hundred years ago. Crazy—bet they flew those carpenters in

63

from the States, instead of letting the islanders build the real thing. Let's go ashore, see what's shaking."

"Tomorrow: I'll stay here," I said, not really listening to him, my ears straining for the sound of a Luger in the clear night.

CHAPTER 5

As Eddie went about securing the sails, straightening the deck, I sat in the cockpit like a mope—staring at the islet, although I could barely see the faint silhouette of the few palm tree tops against the stars.

When Eddie was pulling in our dink, to go ashore, a boat came out from the beach, its motor muffled, passed the DOUBLE-TAKE and came along side. Herb McCarthy, wearing plaid shorts and a hooded knit shirt, tossed Eddie a rope—stepped up on the cutter. "Good to see you chaps. Must have just come in, We've been in daily wireless contact with our Papeete office—can't understand there not being any news on Ruita yet."

"I know, we been listening to the radio, too," Eddie said, shaking the director's hand. "You didn't bring her here, did you?"

Herb pumped my hand—with the knit parka around his face, he really looked like an old pug waiting to work out. "Ray, old man. Come now lads, you can't mean that—but if you wish, we'll smuggle Ruita into the States—once she's found. Told you before, we'll do anything we can to help."

"Thanks, Herbie," I said.

"Don't have to say it's been bloody hell on you, Ray—you're the picture of depressed husband. Don't wish to sound like a ruddy cluck, but cheer up—it will all end jolly well. In the news stories we've already planted—strongly—

that it may have been self-defense: Kitty was heard to threaten Ruita. Lot of wind, but it might help."

I nodded, wondering if he had the pearl on him. Herb had told me every cent he could beg and borrow was sunk in the picture: was he desperate enough to kill for a gem he thought was worth half a hundred grand?

"Where's Matt—everybody?" Eddie asked.

"Sleeping. Matt has to be up at 4:30 A.M., sit in the make-up chair for an hour, go over his lines. He's a lousy study, but works hard to be up on his lines. Chaps, with this wonderful early light, so clear and sharp, things have been going splendidly—already have six reels in the can, nearly a week ahead of our shooting schedule. If we can keep the pace, mean a savings of over $125,000.—a neat piece of cake. Ruita was so right about poor Kitty—she never would have looked the Polynesian queen, but Rosa—perfect! You know, being Mexican, she has Indian blood."

"Who hasn't?" Eddie asked.

McCarthy laughed. "I'm far too bushed for an argument. Do come aboard the schooner for a night cap with me? Only way I can relax after a day behind the cameras."

"We're kind of pooped ourselves. Have some liquor of yours in the hold, unload them tomorrow . . ."

"Keep them down there for the time being. Don't want too much booze around when Matt's working. Sorry you won't join me in a belt, but . . ."

"Come on, Eddie, let's go aboard for a drink," I cut in as Eddie raised his cockeyed eyebrows at me in surprise. The last thing I wanted was a drink and Herb's clipped hot air . . . but there wasn't any point sitting on my rusty: we were here to find a murderer and the sooner we started, the quicker Ruita and I could be back to the peace of Numega.

Eddie double-checked the anchor, then we jumped into McCarthy's skiff and a moment later were drinking Irish whiskey in the lounge of the DOUBLE-TAKE. Herbie showed us a closet lined with tin-sheeting, six metal cans of film on the floor. He said, "Trying something new—no rushes. Hell of a chance, but developing here, or in Tahiti is too risky. We were going to fly it to the States, once a week, but I've decided to wait, take it all back on the boat. One plane accident . . . well, I'm an old fashioned bloke,

65

no confidence in planes. This negative is literally worth more than its weight in gold. Tell you, I've never had a picture come off so smashingly . . ."

"You all living on the schooner?" I asked, innocently.

"Yes, including Rosa, the head cameraman, the featured players. Set up a couple of tents for the others, and a large mess tent. Andy, the ship's cook, doing a jolly job of feeding——having bangers and mash for breakfast tomorrow, join us."

Eddie asked. "What the hell's that?"

"Sausages and mashed potatoes, you heathen. Say, wait till you see the boat set we've built on the beach——an inspiration."

"Saw it from the HOOKER," Eddie said. "Just the stern, isn't it?"

"At first we were going to build an exact duplicate of Wallis' ship, THE DOLPHIN, but that costs like hell. Most of the scenes take place ashore, so next we considered shooting the few boat shots in the studio, using a process background. But this——not only cheaper, also far more realistic——having this stern section built right on the edge of the water, on rockers, we have real sky and the bloody Pacific in the background. Of course, a storm would sink our set, but the weather has been simply. . . ."

Standing beside an open porthole, I sipped my whiskey, ears straining for the sound of a shot from the islet. In my dizzy mind I tried to picture the cabin layout of the schooner. Herbie helped matters by taking us down to his cabin to see some still shots, putting a finger across his mouth like a child as we walked by the curtained doorways of the other cabins——hearing snoring, even-breathing, wind-breaking.

With a corny leer, I whispered, "This Rosa sharing Matt's cabin?"

"Stop it, Ray. When Matt's working, he's all business—— his coin is riding on this picture, too."

We switched to warm rum in his cabin as McCarthy showed us the stills. The Mexican actress was beautiful but, somehow, looked too 'exotic,' too much the dream girl. There were nude and bare breasted photos of Titin diving into the ocean, one of Rosa naked under a waterfall. "Use the bare-ass stuff in the foreign prints, and for publicity

66

shots in the men's mags. Here—this was taken from our blooming stern prop. You're sailors, defy you to say this doesn't look like an actual sailing vessel. Even the rigging is perfect in every detail. . . ."

Three rums later, when McCarthy had talked himself into a stupor—he really must have been tired to take on such a fast load—Eddie and I swam back to the HOOKER. Eddie went to sleep while I drew a rough plan of the schooner's cabins, then wrapped myself in a blanket atop the cabin, facing the islet and Ruita.

I was awakened at 4 A.M. by a burst of activity on the DOUBLE-TAKE. Lights were on in all the cabins and two skiffs kept ferrying people to the beach. Studying the islet in the misty dawn through Eddie's glasses, I couldn't see a sign of my wife, had to fight the idea of rowing over to see how she was.

Eddie came up on deck, yawning and grumbling about all the noise. Urinating over the side, he waited a moment —scratching his thick head of black hair, then took his morning toilet by swimming under the HOOKER. I followed, the cool shock of the water making me feel better. We went ashore to find the entire island population happily holding paper plates, standing in line for breakfast. There was an "executive" table at one side of the mess tent, where Matt, Walt, Herb, Rosa, and a few others were eating. Matt was knocking off a salad of fresh fruits sprinkled with brightly colored vitamin pills, puffing on a new corncob between bites. We shook hands with everybody, got a cup of coffee and some greasy sausages. Monsieur Clichy was busy rushing about the tent in a yellowed linen suit, wispy beard flowing. He introduced us to Bonten, Chief of Roogona, a sturdy six-footer with iron-grey hair . . . Clichy first explaining about Eddie's "Lion Face," then going into great detail about our part in the battle on Von Rumple's schooner—a yarn which by now was already one of the greatly exaggerated island legends.

Buddy, the fruit with the shaved dome, kept glancing at his watch, reminding Herb they couldn't chance starting shooting until the seaplane arrived. Matt, and the other actors, went to a make-up tent and soon he was sporting a black wig with the hair tied in a knot behind his head, like a matador's pigtail, red silk pantaloons, an open and sleeveless black leather blouse, shiny knee-high boots; brown powder giving Matt's tanned face an odd color—and his teeth painted a kind of blue-white. Rosa Marino not only looked prettier than her photographs, but far better without make-up. By 6 A.M. the morning was bright with early sun and the flying boat landed with a roar and splash. McCarthy shouted, "Okay, everybody on set now!" Matt, Walt, and Rosa—in a fetching *pareu* of gold and silver cloth—rode in a jeep which sped along the beach. Everybody else walked the mile to the set. McCarthy stayed behind for a few minutes to talk to a couple of intense-looking young men from the plane, glancing at newspapers, cost sheets, and other papers. The jeep returned to take them to the "village of Papeete." Far as I could see, the entire crew of the DOUBLE-TAKE was on shore.

I walked with a group of islanders, all of us stopping to admire the ship's stern built on the beach—really a hell of a good job, even to the weathered-coloring of the hull planks. When I reached the set, McCarthy was sitting beside a camera as Rosa and Matt were getting ready to do a love scene in front of a hut. Make-up men flitted around the both of them, and Molly Watson, perched on a stool beside McCarthy—and the only woman on the island to be completely dressed—was pointing to the hut and to something in the script.

A table was removed from the interior of the hut and then Matt strode over to Walt, who handed him a 100 pound barbell. Breathing hard through his open mouth, Matt lifted the weight a dozen times. Eddie, leaving Titin, pushed his way through the admiring crowd, whispered, "Ray, he's cleaning and pressing the barbell—to puff his muscles. Think of everything, don't they?"

"Yeah. Listen, I'm going to search the cabins on the yacht. If you see anybody heading out for the boat, give me a signal . . . eh . . . yell out as though you thought I was on the HOOKER."

"We'll both search the yacht."

"No, if we're both missing from this show, might look odd. Won't take me long." I headed back toward the real village as somebody bawled through a loudspeaker, "Everybody settle down—take your places. No noise—this is a take!" Bonten, the chief, repeated this in the island dialect

68

to the giggling people—sternly warning them no more canned foods would be given to the next person who made a sound. At the same time I heard Herbie's clipped voice screaming, "There's a goddamn hot spot on the hut wall— dull that bright flower!"

The babel of words turned to dead silence and I heard the little bark of the clap board, then Matt's booming voice gushing, "My dear beloved princess. . . ."

Rowing out to the HOOKER, I passed the big schooner and called out, "Ahoy there."

There wasn't any answer and I tied the dink to the HOOKER, swam over to the DOUBLE-TAKE. I made a lot of noise on the deck, shaking the water off—to be certain I was alone on the ship. Happily the cabins were unlocked, the bunks made-up: meaning the steward wouldn't return any time soon. I went over Matt's cabin first—trying to figure where I'd hide something small as a pearl. I searched the drawers under his bunk, clothes, toilet articles, shoes—careful to replace everything I moved. I felt of the carpet edges, the shade of the ceiling light. Walt Sing's room and McCarthy's got the same treatment.

I was completely puzzled—the pearl would hardly be left in the ship's safe, if there was one, or in any public place on the schooner. Nor could I picture Matt—with his change of costumes—carrying it on him. Both Walt and Herb had been wearing shorts and polo shirts—easy enough to hide a pearl in them—but in the sweating heat of the day, I doubted that, too. Of course, the pearl could have already been sent to the States, or even left in Tahiti . . . but I couldn't see myself, or the killer, parting with what he thought was worth fifty grand; not after killing to get it.

There wasn't any point in shaking down Rosa's cabin, but I went through it carefully, then the head cameraman's: I searched all the cabins. In Molly Watson's I saw a picture on the dresser of her and Matt—obviously taken years ago. Matt looked like a teen-ager. Leaving her cabin—pulling the curtain over the doorway—I heard the muffled sound of sneakers, turned to see a sailor rushing at me.

Before I could say a word, he started swinging. I threw a right which missed. His didn't, but he was a little, wiry joker, and although his fist bounced smack off my chin, it

69

merely staggered me. "I was only looking . . . for . . . the head," I gasped, trying to clinch.

"Ya robbing bastid!" he yelled, punching my stomach as if beating a drum. I set myself, doubled him up with a neat right right to his gut. As he jack-knifed double, I heard footsteps behind me. Before I could turn, a knife seemed to cut my head cleanly off my neck. My noggin flew straight up, hit the metal underside of the deck above with a crash of blinding lights . . . and the rest of me took off from a launching pad.

When I came to—probably minutes later—two crewmen were standing over me; the guy I'd hit and an even smaller man in a blue slack suit who was holding a thin, blackjack. Foolishly, I rubbed the back of my neck and screamed with the pain—a high yell jarring the cobwebs from my tired brains. The one with the blackjack drawled, "You sit right there, old buddy, and be nice. . . . Now, now, don't you move—*sit!*

The other crew member, rubbing his stomach, said, "Give me that sap, I'll work this big bastid over until. . . . !"

"You just take it slow. You call ashore?"

"Aha. The Chink is coming out."

"I told you about that before; best not let Mr. Sing hear you say that—he take you apart and spit you out with his Judo. Okay, let's all be quiet and no more trouble."

"I was looking for the head," I began, my own words making my head ring. Every few seconds my noggin started to hover above me, while the back of my throbbing neck was so swollen I expected the skin to burst.

"Now, old buddy, even if John here mistook you for one of the thieving natives; you're off that HOOKER, know your way around ships—a john wouldn't ever have a *curtained* doorway."

I heard Eddie calling me from the beach and seconds later the sound of a motor as the skiff edged along side. Walt and McCarthy came running down to us. The director yelled, "You bloody idiots—who hit Mr. Judson?"

"We come out in one of the native canoes, sir. John here, found him snooping around the cabins and being so brown and in shorts, thought he was stealing. He belted John, so I sapped him."

Walt pulled me to my feet, asked, "Are you okay, Ray?"

"Only trying to do my duty, sir," the blackjack man whined.

"All right, both of you, on with your ruddy work. Forget it," Herb McCarthy said.

The three of us walked to the lounge. Although my head kept trying to soar away from my neck, I walked okay. Seeing magazines on the lounge table, I said, "Don't blame the crewmen, it must have looked to them as if I was a sneak-thief. I swam over to read your new magazines, was hunting for the head . . ."

"Of course. Sit down, Ray," Herb said. Walt poured me a drink of brandy. It was strong stuff, burning my throat—clearing my head.

McCarthy rubbed his nose as he sat on the table. It seemed to me his hands were shaking. "Ray, actual movie making requires all-out attention. Interruptions like this are not only costly, but break the creative mood of. . . ."

"You sound as if you think I *was* stealing!" I said, righteous anger in my voice—I actually didn't want the damn pearl, merely to learn *who* had the gem.

The director waved his hands. "Ray, I understand how you feel, your lovely Ruita suspected of murder. Perhaps you were looking for the john—perhaps snooping around. If the latter, I can't fault you, but it's imperative we have an immediate understanding. Ruita is still getting title credit as technical adviser, which should prove to you we're her friends—and your's. I don't wish to order you off the DOUBLE-TAKE, or location, you're still on our payroll, too, you know. But I have more than enough on my blooming mind bringing this pix in. In short, Ray, stop playing detective; it isn't necessary, we're on your side."

"That's a fact, Ray," Walt Sing added, glancing at his wrist watch.

I felt like a fool—for being caught. "Herb, I . . . was snooping. My wife has vanished. I . . . well . . . had to assure myself she wasn't aboard."

"Of course, Ray. I have to rush back—we're setting up for a new scene. Make you feel any better, I'll leave orders you can search the ship from bow to stern. I mean that, Ray."

"I'm finished. By the way, is Molly Watson Matt's mother?"

71

McCarthy and Walt looked flabbergasted, then Herb asked, "What ever gave you that way-out idea?"

"A picture of the two of them in her cabin."

The director actually shook with laughter and even Walt smiled. When he quieted down, McCarthy said, "Oh Lord, if it wouldn't get Molly in a rage—and her sugar has been acting up again—be the best fun bit I've heard this month. Molly was Matt's first wife! She's about seven years older than Matt, looks like homemade hell—now . . . but his *mother!*"

"She was his wife?" I repeated.

"The old story; a fading, small time actress infatuated with a pretty boy. His career on the rise, Molly's never was headed any place. They divorce, she takes to the bottle, becomes sickly. True, Molly has become a damn good script girl, but Matt keeps her on the payroll as a sentimental gesture, a kind streak under all those muscles which. . . ."

"I know, part of the All-American-Man-Image," I cut in.

McCarthy shrugged. "You're entirely wrong, chap, strictly no publicity on this. It's true kindness, he helped Molly beat the booze." Walt Sing glanced at his watch again. Herb stood up. "Well, back to the grind. Hope to get in three more takes before the light fades. Want a lift to the HOOKER, or the beach?"

"Swim back, help my head," I said as we reached the deck. "Where was Molly when Kitty was killed?"

"Ray, stop beating a dead horse—the police checked us all. She was working on the script in the hotel office. Matter of fact, I saw her typing there—off and on."

While they roared back to the beach in the skiff, I dived overboard, my neck throbbing again as I hit the water. Once on the HOOKER I studied the islet through Eddie's glasses —without seeing any sign of Ruita. Seconds later the skiff came racing back toward the HOOKER, with Eddie at the wheel. When he jumped on deck and I told him what had happened, Eddie grunted, "I didn't see, or hear, the crew using a canoe. His wife? That mean anything to us?"

I shrugged and the back of my neck bloomed with pain again. "At least I've planted the idea strongly—that we don't know where Ruita is. On the bad side—the damn pearl isn't in any of the cabins."

72

"Pearl's easy to hide, Ray. What do we do now?"

"I don't know—wait, see what breaks, I guess. I've another idea going: know those cans of exposed film Herb showed us on the DOUBLE-TAKE? If they were stolen, now, they'd have to start the picture all over again—be a hell of an expense."

The puzzled look on Eddie's battered face became a big grin. "With the cans of negative we could blackmail 'em into giving us the real killer! Hey, now that's great . . . if they actually know who did it. Jeez, deal like that, they'd blow a mile high, might try knocking us off, have us arrested . . . is it piracy to rob a ship in a harbor, or only on the high seas?"

"Forget it, for now. Merely an idea. My head is killing me."

"A raw fish will reduce the swelling," Eddie said, taking a knife and diving over the side.

I kept the fish on the back of my neck until both of us began to stink; even slept for a few hours, although I could hardly wait for darkness, a chance to see Ruita, discuss things with her.

Around 6 P.M. I went ashore to join Eddie in the mess tent. After eating, everybody—islanders and movie people, took their last bath and swim for the day—except Molly Watson; she sat in the rear of the mess tent, busy typing script changes under a dim, flicking, oil light. She sure looked an old hag in the odd shadows.

Both Matt and Herb came out of the ocean to ask how I was feeling. I said I was okay, going to do a little night fishing. Almost on a silent cue, Walt appeared to hand Matt a new corncob. The actor said, "Like to join you, Ray, I love fishing. But need plenty of shut-eye when working—so my eyes will have that big sparkle the next day. What a creepy way for a grown man to earn his bread!"

Leaving Eddie ashore on his usual nightly quest—trying to find a girl—soon as it grew dark I pushed off in the dink —rowing away from the islet, then doubling back in the darkness; rowing fast as I could without leaving a wake. Reaching the islet I beached the dink, whispered, "Ruita?"

There wasn't any answer. I called again. From the darkness she whispered, "Darling, take off your clothes."

"What?"

Stepping out of a shadow into the edge of the pale moonlight, my wife was beautiful beyond belief in her nakedness. Smiling softly, she told me, "Ray, all day I have been thinking of your coming here, making love as my ancestors did —two nude people."

"Honey, there's no time for. . . ."

"Undress, dearest! This isn't the cruel *popaa* world of sexual sin and hypocrisy—but *our* world where there must always be time for love. Take off your shirt, drop your pants—quickly. I've thought many hours of this moment."

She vanished back into the shadows. I tore my things off, ran to my wife with a sob of joy.

Later, lying in the lean-to of pleated palm leaves Ruita had made, I told her what had happened, my idea of stealing the cans of negative. Stroking my face, her thumb playing with the stubble of hair on my chin, she said thoughtfully, "No, they could jail you and then where would we be? As Eddie said, they may not know the real killer."

"I'm sure they all know a damn sight more than they let on. We're getting no place, have to do something drastic."

"Maybe you found something important: this Molly. With a first wife always some spark of real love remains. Seems odd she would be content to sit by and watch Matt make a fool of himself with all these other women. Now we have another motive for the murder—jealousy.

"Jealousy? Matt pays no attention to Molly, treats her as just another employee."

Ruita stretched, moved her nipples against my chest. "Jealousy on *her* part. Even when I am old and wrinkled, I will fiercely resent you looking at another woman."

"According to Herb, she has an alibi for the time of the murder. The pearl wasn't in her cabin—but since she doesn't swim, could be she has it on her person. If it was only jealousy, why would she take the pearl?"

"Perhaps to make it appear a robbery . . . I don't know. Molly—she's the diabetic, isn't she?"

"Yeah."

"At least we can learn if she has the gem—or if the others are carrying it around. Ray, in the morning talk to Clichy, this French storekeeper you told me about. Casually mention you're interested in buying any large pearls he may know about. Say you have cash, but things must be kept quiet—afraid you might be robbed if it was known you carried much money. Now, at this big tent where everybody eats, you and Eddie start a discussion—small talk spreads like a tide—about it is bad for pearls to be in contact with a person *all* the time. Especially those people with high blood pressure, acid, sugar. This is not actually so, although it would temporarily spoil the lustre, for pearls do react to the blood's temperature and content. Tell them a tall story—you heard a pearl worth a great deal of money was carried around by a man with a high acid condition of the blood, when he went to sell it months later—the pearl was in such poor condition it was worthless. Chances are, there is nobody in Roogona who knows enough about pearls to contradict . . ."

"Then Molly will panic, hide the pearl in her cabin!"

"She, or whoever has the pearl may either hide it—or try to sell it to Monsieur Clichy. That should be sufficient evidence for the police."

Kissing her roughly, I whispered, "You ruin the old saying about beauty and no brains."

"Another empty *popaa* expression," Ruita mumbled, crushing my lips with hers.

When I was leaving I asked if she wanted anything; food, water. "Ray, it is said—in the shade of a coconut tree a Polynesian will never want—but tomorrow night, do bring me some books, something to read. Otherwise, I think so much about you . . . I may swim to the cutter one of these afternoons . . . *Here vau ia oe,* Ray!"

I repeated, "I love you!" in Tahitian, and didn't leave until I heard the generators start on the movie set—so happily exhausted I barely was able to row back to the HOOKER before dawn lit up the horizon.

CHAPTER 6

The Frenchman's store was shut in the morning—the entire village came to a stop, everybody watching the movie-making, whether they were extras in the scene or not. I managed to get Clichy aside before they broke for lunch. Eddie and I had decided it would be a smart move to let him know the pearl might solve the Papeete murder, bring favorable attention to him in Paris—always the dream of the forgotten, island civil servant.

Before I could even hint at it, Monsieur Clichy told me, "This motion picture is a great thing for Roogona. Not merely the material gifts to the islanders, but Monsieur McCarthy assures me when the film is shown in Paris, news stories and photos of the island will appear in the papers. It will acquaint the Home Office with Roogona . . . perhaps a Legion of Honor ribbon for my humble self. Ay, it is indeed something one could never plan for. Now, what supplies do you wish to purchase, Monsieur Judson?"

"Pearls."

His gaunt face, skin tight as old parchment and yellower than his shirt, the drooping eyes—all turned into an almost comical mask of astonishment. "I have no pearls, monsieur."

"In case you *ever* hear of any large gems, the rare rainbows, the silver-blue pearls, let me know. I am ready to pay a good price—cash, plus a generous commission."

"But . . . I may not hear of such a pearl in years. This is not . . ."

"There's no rush. Who knows, you may hear of a gem within the next second, too. That is how it goes with

76

pearls." It occurred to me I'd never seen Clichy swimming, taking the nightly bath.

Tugging at his dirty beard, he nodded. "I have heard you raise pearls on Numega."

"We experimented with them, my wife and I."

"Ah yes, your wife. Word of the Papeete killing has spread, of course. Bad business. Myself, I do not believe an islander would kill, murder is one of our few civilized vices these people haven't adopted. Well, should I ever hear of such pearls, I will get word to you on Numega, or to Papeete."

"Thank you. Oh, one thing more—this is between us only. If it should be known I carry much cash—with so many *popaas* on Roogona now, they might be tempted to rob me. You understand, Monsieur Clichy?"

"Indeed, Monsieur Judson, you are most wise. I shall keep it a business secret." We shook hands and I walked over to the mess tent.

The rest of the act was almost too easy: islanders love to talk and Eddie was already off and running about a "fellow in Samoa" who had found a large pearl while diving for shell, kept it in his belt all the time. His wife urged him to sell it but he was waiting until he went to Australia, to receive a higher price. He had died of a "sour stomach," and the pearl had died too, turning a sickly grey.

Chief Bonten said this was truly so . . . people who ate too much out of cans, not the fresh fruits and fish which had kept their ancestors strong—such people had poor blood, and should not be allowed in the same hut with pearls.

I kept watching Molly Watson, the others, at the "executive" table, wondering how much they understood of the island dialect. Molly nibbled her food slowly, showing no reaction: Matt was eating a huge coconut salad, talking to McCarthy—both pointing to some cost sheets. Walt was listening to them, while Rosa Marino was whispering to the head cameraman.

Like a good straight man, Eddie asked me loudly—in English—"Ray, you know about pearls, isn't it true they are *living* gems?"

"Yes. For example, it is not good for pearls to be exposed to the strong sun too long, nor kept entirely in the darkness of a box. It destroys their lustre, which is what makes pearls valuable. Like human skin, pearls must also be cleaned—and with the most delicate of soaps. Anybody with too much acid or sugar in their blood wearing a string of pearls around their neck, or carrying them in their pocket for days, would cause the pearls to turn dull, lose most of their value." As I talked I glanced at the "executive" table: everybody there acted as if they couldn't care less.

We kept it going for four days—each night I told Ruita how the islanders had enlarged on yarns they had once heard. An old man allegedly remembered his grandmother telling him of a whaler who had been her lover—stolen a large pearl from her, she having no idea in the old days of its real value. "This evil man had too much blood in him, suffered a stroke on the long voyage home. He died two days after reaching the famous city of Boston. His wife found the pearl in his clothes, rushed out to sell it. . . . The pearl had been worth many hundreds of 'bird money'—the big silver dollars used in the old days. Now, having lost its color from the bad blood of the man, it was so worthless, his angry wife threw it into his grave with him."

McCarthy asked about 'bird money,' and I repeated the whole tale in English—while explaining that the old Mexican silver dollars used in trade then, had a big eagle on them. Nobody showed any reaction, except mild interest—Molly's pale face looking bored. Matt went off on a yarn of a South African who swallowed an uncut diamond, to smuggle it out of the mine, and died in torture when the rock became stuck in his gut.

By the third day, after thoroughly searching all the yacht cabins again, I felt we were wasting time. Eddie and I talked over the idea of the HOOKER 'slipping anchor' during the morning, bumping the schooner and giving me a chance to remove the negative cans, force a showdown. Nor had I forgotten my other 'plan'—to settle on some deserted island. Ruita was dead set against both ideas, thought them childish, and said so.

Depressed, I was back to the feeling of living in a jerky nightmare . . . seeing Matt swagger around in 200-year-old clothes—actually looking the part of an 18th century adventurer . . . gave me an unreal feeling. Plus, I was moving

78

about in an exhausted daze; every night Ruita and I made frantic love—as if it might be our last night—while during the day I had to stay awake to make small talk about pearls and sickness, listen to inflated lies about gems. Trying to play detective was discouraging, I was far from certain the pearl had any real meaning in the murder.

On the afternoon of the fourth day as I was lounging on the coral dock, my tired mind going over various remote islands—the reasons some of them were deserted—lack of water, in the hurricane path, even fallout—I had dozed off when a small hand shook me. Opening my eyes, I saw Clichy's dirty beard fluttering above me.

"Monsieur Judson, I *have a pearl!*" he whispered. "A pearl so large and full of color it blinds the eyes!"

"Who's selling it?"

"I am."

"You? Where did you get it? What kind of a pearl?"

"A rainbow! I am not at liberty to say where I got it. What does it matter? I am not acting as a middleman, you understand—I have bought the gem, it is mine!"

"Okay. Where is it now?" I asked, getting up, trying to think clearly—certain he was lying, didn't have enough ready cash to have purchased the gem.

"I will have it—for your inspection. I trust you are prepared to pay much cash money, Monsieur Judson?"

I nodded. "Did you mention my name?"

"Monsieur still does not understand—*I now own the pearl.* I am a businessman, not a fool. Certainly I did not mention you—give the seller a choice of buyers. For the very same reasons you wished your money a secret, I have kept it quiet—about having such a fabulous gem in my possession."

"It's at your store?"

"Where I have the pearl is known only to me. You state when you wish to examine it, I shall produce the pearl."

"Tonight. 7:30, in your rooms."

"Good. Remember, cash, Monsieur Judson."

I watched Clichy walk away, the almost girlish prance to his short steps. I found Eddie busy talking to a giggling Titin, on the outskirts of the crowd watching a realistic fight scene between Matt and two other actors. Titin now wore—while any scene was being shot—a comical 'sack' dress she had picked up in Papeete, sheer stockings, and fuzzy red slippers—to impress upon her friends she was an actress. The moment shooting was done for the day, Titin rushed to wrap a *pareu* around her perfect body, kick off her slippers.

When I told Eddie, "We have to go—to the HOOKER. Something's . . . eh . . . come up!"

He told me, in English, "Just when I'm making time . . . something else has to come up."

"Goddamnit, this is urgent!"

"Okay, okay. . . . Let's go, I can see on your face it's important." Turning to Titin, he told her there was a leak on the boat, added something in the island dialect I didn't get.

Rowing out to the HOOKER, neither of us talked—even whispers carry on the water. But once inside the cabin I explained the deal, added, "Whoever approached Clichy certainly didn't leave the pearl with him—that would be dumb. Also, I doubt if he has the cash to buy it. So, around twilight—when the island is bathing—either Clichy will go to the seller, or—more likely—they'll bring the gem to his store. He'll tell them to return shortly, after he sees me, for the money. We . . ."

"We keep an eye on him or anyboody approaching his place. Then what—jump Molly?"

"We'll have the dink on the sand, past the bathing beach. We carry her to the dink, row to the islet—I want a complete story, all the details, before we make our next move. If we have to belt her, be careful."

"I like the idea, on the quiet of the islet, she'll spill, then we call in Clichy, as the island official, and Chief Bonten, to arrest her—do it all before Matt or Herbie can use any fast talk or influence."

Clichy's store was the biggest building on Roogona, except for the church. The shop was a ramshackle affair of palm boards, tin can roof, with a thatched hut added to the rear of the store for living quarters. A path of crushed burnt coral lined with empty Coke bottles, led from the dirt "main street" to the worn steps of his shop. A few shade palm trees ringed the store, with other huts less than 50 feet away.

Eddie simply went into the nearest hut on the left of the

store, talked for awhile, then said he was sleepy—with true island hospitality a mat was unrolled for him . . . giving Eddie a perfect view of the store. I went into a hut on the other side of the shop and after some banal chatter with a toothless old crone about the weather, asked if I could sleep for awhile, was politely offered a pandanus mat.

In the next few hours I saw only islanders come to the shop. As twilight darkened the sky, grandma—now joined by her grandson and his plump wife—announced they were going for a swim. Yawning like a ham actor, I said I'd wait for their return, assured them I didn't need a lamp.

After a few minutes Clichy closed the screen door of his shop and seconds later an oil lamp was lit in his rooms. He had a swank hut—real glass windows. As best I could judge by the greyness of the sky, the single bright star—it had to be after 7 P.M. The . . .

I heard the sound of footsteps, soft pad of sneakered feet, Buddy came trotting along the "main street," his skin and shaved dome gleaming wet in the dim light. He wore only sneakers and swim trunks. As he turned into the coral path, I saw a little white box in his right hand. I was confused— he hadn't even been in Papeete when Kitty was killed.

Buddy peered into the dark screen door as I walked over to him. Eddie came up from the other side. Buddy said, "Oh, Ray—gave me a nasty start, pussyfooting up behind me like . . . Hello, Eddie."

"Want something in the store, Buddy?" I asked.

"Sort of." He held up a little plastic pill box. "The Frenchman makes up a medicine, or something, for Molly. She'll call for the pills later when. . . ."

"Molly sent you?" Eddie asked.

"Aha. The old girl's at the dock, not feeling at all well, so I said I'd. . . ."

I grabbed the pill box from his slim hand as he asked, "What the hell are you. . . . ?" Eddie's hook quieted him.

Opening the tiny box, I pulled aside some cotton, my fingers feeling the hard smoothness . . . as Eddie lit a match. It was a perfect rainbow pearl the size of a small grape and even in the harsh matchlight—the pearl was a number of delicate shades of wonderful colors. Sucking in his breath, Eddie grunted, "Man, what a bubble! That's the largest. . . ."

81

I slammed the little box shut, shoved it in my pocket. As we ran toward the dock, I asked, "How long will baldy be a study in still life?"

"Couple of minutes. Sorry to wallop the poor bastard."

Some 500 islanders and *popaas* were horsing around in the water near the dock. Molly Watson was sitting on a wooden crate, a shawl on thin shoulders, looking very small and pathetic in the faint light. The moment she saw us, she jumped to run, but I was right on top of her. "I have your pills, Miss Watson."

"I don't know what the devil you're talking about." There was a nervous shrillness to the strong voice.

"Good, because we're going to talk it over," I said, picking her up, muffling a scream with my hand over the thin lips, feeling the teeth bite into my palm. I started running along the beach with her. She was slapping and kicking me; some of the islanders pointed at us. Eddie shouted, "Since she never swims—we throw her in!"

This bright crack brought laughter, but one of the movie crew—the head grip—came splashing out of the water. "Cut the horseplay, Judson, Molly isn't feeling well."

Eddie's left sent him spinning like a drunk, then flat on the dark sand. All told, I had to run about 200 yards before I saw the dink; was panting like a rusty engine. Tossing the anchor in, Eddie pushed the boat out. Stepping in with Molly, I nearly capsized the little boat—Molly stopped fighting, lay in my arms—about 100 pounds of dead weight . . . except for her eyes: they were full of cold fury.

Rowing hard, Eddie said, "Maybe in the twilight nobody saw me hit that guy—maybe! Getting dark so fast they won't know where we're going, probably figure out to the HOOKER!"

My fingers were wet—I realized Molly was weeping. Loosening my hand over her mouth, I told her, "Don't try anything—it's too late."

She mumbled something about my mother's sex life—her lips moving, hot and slimy against my hand—then Molly continued her silent weeping.

Ruita stepped out of the shadows as we landed on the islet. Standing Molly on her feet, I told my wife, "She had the pearl!" and yanked the pill box out of my pocket.

I pushed Molly down on the sand, so the moon acted as

82

a faint spotlight on her pale face; Eddie, Ruita and I remained in the shadows. I said, "Molly, we want the truth about Kitty's murder! I don't want to hurt you, but my wife's involved, and if you make us learn the truth the hard way, we'll do it. Might keep you here for a few days without your diabetes' pills, for example. All we want is the truth about. . . ."

"You don't have to third degree me," Molly cut in, voice low and clear. "I never meant to involve Ruita—or anybody else. I'd read about the use of *cerbera* poison while checking historical facts in the script, found the trees growing in Tahiti. I thought . . . they wouldn't be able to trace it in her blood, that her death would be called a heart attack, or due to causes unknown. Didn't think the island police would be that sharp."

"Why did you kill her?" Ruita asked. "Jealous?"

Molly stared up at us, then laughed—deep laughter almost like a man's. "Jealous of that piece of baggage? Good God no! I'm a sickly woman, a dying woman with a year or less to live. I wanted to *live* my last months . . . wanted money! Money rightfully mine—I was the one who discovered Matt, a multi-million dollar property! I guided him to stardom, I . . . I kept pleading with him to give me enough money to live in comfort, but the big bastard tossed me a job—have me around to rub his success in my face! Before we left Hollywood my doc told me the news—cancer. In Papeete I again begged Matt for money—not much—I only asked for ten grand. I even showed him the doc's cancer report. In a maudlin moment he agreed—claimed he was waiting for money from the States, would have it by the time he returned from your island." Her voice became a hoarse whisper. "You know the rest."

"You tell us," I said softly.

"The louse changed his mind! I knew the money had come for him but when he returned from Numega he said I'd have to wait until the picture was released and new money started coming in, that he was busted. The pix won't return money for at least a year from now—I couldn't wait. Matt told me right to my face he'd spent the money buying a pearl for Kitty—she was blackmailing him. Wished to God I knew what she had on him . . . ! I went to her room, told her about my condition, asked her to give me the pearl

83

——she could get more from Matt, the idiot belives his own publicity slop about being the world's great lover. Oh, I didn't expect her to give it to me, but I was desperate. She was strutting around in the nude, flaunting her youth in my face——me, who once had more beauty and talent in my little finger than this little whore even knew existed! She was playing her crazy records, hardly heard me. We had a fight, but being sickly, Kitty threw me out. The rest . . ." Molly waved her thin hands in the moonlight. "I knew the bellhops often left her food. . . . I found a *cerbera* tree, squeezed the milky juice into the coconut drink on the serving table outside her door. Then I waited a half hour, went to her room. She was dead . . . I found the pearl. . . ."

Over the low monotone of words tumbling from her thin lips, we heard another sound——the roar of the skiff approaching the islet at full speed. I glanced at Eddie: he was smiling, head cocked as he listened intently. I started to move toward Molly, but Eddie put his hand on my shoulder ——shook his head.

". . . The pearl was said to be worth fifty grand or more. I was going to sell it, spend my last months traveling—— leisurely, quietly. I've been on such a goddamn merry-go-round all my life, hustling, scrawling for success, a buck. . . ." Molly stopped, the night full of the launch's powerful motor.

Eddie said, "They're dumb as hell, speeding on this reef."

From a distance, in the island dialect, a man shouted, "Slow! Slow . . . !"

With the almost perfect timing of a play, his yell was interrupted by a splintering crash, and violent curses——in English. Holding Molly gently by her elbow, I walked the dozen or so feet to the other side of the islet. About ten yards out, Matt, McCarthy, and Sing, were standing in the submerged skiff, a hell of a hole in its bow.

Monsieur Clichy and Bonten were padding around them in an outrigger canoe. As Matt started to dive——the Frenchman yelled, "No, no! You will cut yourself to pieces on the coral!"

Matt dived——a perfect shallow dive——swam towards us. Bonten paddled the canoe close enough for Walt and Herb to jump in——warning them to move slowly or they would all be swamped. As Matt came out of the ocean, bellowing, "What the dirty hell are you doing to Molly!" he sounded like one of his star roles—looked the part, too—silver hair flashing in the moonlight, wet pants and polo shirt clinging to his muscular frame—blood on one thigh—from the razor sharp coral . . . his swaggering walk.

"Don't come too near," Eddie said. "Walt ain't here to run interference for you."

He stopped on the edge of the beach, flexing his long arms as he shook water off his head—waiting for the others to paddle ashore. Suddenly pointing to Molly, his voice projecting like thunder, Matt asked, "Bitch, what did you tell them?"

Pushing me away, Molly took a few steps toward Matt. "Only what a cheap creep you are!" There was pure hatred in her words.

"The old pitch about how you discovered me?" Matt said, giving us his famous sneer. "She gave you the icing, but not the whole goddamn crumbling cookie! Go on, Molly, tell 'em how you were an extra all your empty life— hungry till you met me! Hard to believe now, but once I really loved this broad. Didn't give a hoot about her being older, all the lovers she'd had in this racket. Back in those days, to me, she was the most beautiful gal on earth! I was willing to work for her, dig ditches, run a gas station—anything. I could have been a big athlete, perhaps an Olympic swimmer, college team scholarships. . . . I was glad to give that all up, just make a living for her, have us a normal life. But she had to make me an actor—no, a goddamn *personality!* Did she hand you the line about how she 'guided' me up the ladder . . . ?"

"Matt, shut up!" McCarthy yelled from the canoe.

". . . Always hear about the casting couch for starlets," Matt went on, voice booming, "but somehow nobody ever writes about the life of a pretty boy in Hollywood . . . all the fat, ugly, wives of the 'right' husbands you have to sleep with, love soggy old women who make you puke with their wretched bodies and stinking breath! You have to really swing, make them think it's *the* love, so they'll nag hubby to give you a fat part. Know who used to find these old biddys for me, who drove me to the hotels, their homes, in our rundown heap? Her—my beloved wife! My . . .' "

85

"Louse, you were anxious to be a star!" Molly screamed. "Like a mutt in heat, straining at the leash—once I pointed out the woman, the . . . !"

Walt and McCarthy came splashing ashore, followed by Bonten and Monsieur Clichy. "This is kidnapping, a most serious offense!" Herbie said, clipping the words. "I will have you all. . . ."

"Don't talk us to death!" I snapped. "Sure, there has been a damn serious offense committed—murder!"

Walt and Herb ran at us, followed by Matt. As Eddie and I stepped forward, the thunder of a shot split the air— we all came to such an abrupt halt, it would have been comical under other circumstances. I turned to see Ruita holding the Luger. She said softly, in Tahitian, "He who wants to live, will stand still!"

Drawing himself to his full five feet, Clichy came sloshing out of the water—nearly stumbling over his wet pants. "Madame, you dare to threaten an official of the Republic, on French soil? I warn you—I hereby order you not to resist!"

Ruita answered in French, "It is because I respect France's long tradition of justice, and your office, that as a French citizen I am helping you carry out justice."

"I am Bonten, Chief of Roogona," the Chief said in broken French. "Let us not have any more trouble."

In Tahitian Ruita told him, "I am happy you are here, for you too, must hear the truth." Turning to Molly, she told her in English, "Tell them what you have told us about Kitty's death."

Molly stood there, silently, for a moment. I shook her elbow. "You've already said it before witnesses—Eddie and I."

Clichy shrilled, "Monsieur, you will not use force on a woman in my presence!"

Shrugging her thin shoulders, Molly said, "Oh, shut up—or talk English! It doesn't matter; I'll never live to be guillotined. Okay—I poisoned Kitty in Papeete. I killed the bitch for a pearl, which should have rightfully been mine. I confess it. There's my confession and you can all shove it!"

Ruita started to translate it into French, but Clichy held up a waxen hand. "I understood." He explained things to Bonten, speaking the island dialect. The Chief nodded gravely, said he was glad an islander hadn't done the murder. Then he added, "This makes a big problem— we have no jail on Roogona. Where will we keep the lady?"

Clichy pulled at his silly beard. "I shall inform Papeete on the wireless. In the meantime, she can live as before, but under house arrest. There is no way for her to leave the island. We will now take her ashore. I will return in another canoe for you." He said this last sentence to Mc-Carthy. Bonten took Molly's hand, then gently picked her up, carried her out to the canoe. Clichy suddenly did a smart about-face, walked over to Ruita, said stiffly, "Firearms are forbidden on Roogona. Also, I will need the pearl, for evidence."

Ruita handed him the pill box and the gun. Clichy walked out into the ankle-deep water, stepped into the canoe—holding the Luger as if he was a general with a sword of surrender.

We watched them paddle into the darkness. Herb Mc-Carthy rubbed his hands, told Matt, "This won't be too bloody. Some dirt, but like that phony rape case didn't hurt you—women fighting over Matt Gregg; it's expected. Damn shame Molly looks so old, but we'll send the press snaps of her taken when she was an actress. The. . . ."

"You lice are about the poorest excuses for men I've ever seen!" I heard myself say, the words trembling with rage. " 'We'll stand by you . . . the company will see to it Ruita gets off. . . .' All the time you must have suspected Molly was the killer!"

"Ray, stop babbling like a child," Herb said calmly. "Certainly, we suspected her, would have gladly thrown Molly to the police—but believe me, our hands were tied. We fully intended to stand by Ruita. . . ."

"While she was in jail? Our life ruined!"

"We had no choice. There's another ruddy factor in this you don't know, and I can't tell. . . ."

"You mean Kitty blackmailing Matt?"

McCarthy stiffened as though I'd socked him, nervously rubbed his flat nose.

"You would have . . . sacrificed . . . me to misery,"

87

Ruita said, disbelief and anger in her voice, "merely because of . . . of poor headlines for him?"

"Beautiful Ruita, listen to me—we're not bloody monsters. We *were* going to hire the best lawyers from Paris, see to it you were given a suspended sentence. Granted, you would have been on the end of some nasty publicity, but that lasts only as long as the next headline. Isolated on Numega, what difference would it really have made to you and Ray?"

"It would have meant the end of me," Matt said. "Not me, as a person; what I stand for. It was ugly blackmail—involving a little boy I turned on, the fool became an addict . . ."

"For God's sake, close your big stupid mouth!" McCarthy cut in. "It would have spoiled the image we've built of Matt—a ten million buck image. Let's forget it—no harm has been done." He turned to Matt again. "We can handle this Frenchman, and I'm sure Ruita, Ray, Eddie, will cooperate. If the . . . eh . . . blackmail angle doesn't come out—we're still in business. Even Molly will understand." McCarthy spun around to me. "Ray, you must realize our position, every cent we have—or will make in the future—the whole packet goes down the drain if Matt's smeared. Now wait, be honest, realistic—in our boots, what would you have done to save millions? I swear, we were going to see to it Ruita wouldn't do time or. . . ."

My wife turned her back, got sick. Stroking her shoulders I told them, "I don't give a fat damn how you handle it, what happens to you! Ruita and I are going back to Numega, and if we ever leave it again—we'll deserve anything we get."

"Fine! Bless you both and thank you!" Herb held out his hand to me. "Eddie, don't you worry, I'll take care of you."

Standing there, the picture of nonchalance, Matt boomed, "As the old gag goes, all's well that ends well."

I pushed McCarthy's hand away so hard he fell. As I stepped toward Matt, Walt Sing dived at me—ran smack into Eddie's left hook, came to a sliding stop on his face in the sand.

Matt backed away. "Ray, I don't want to hurt you . . ."

I heard myself screaming, "The great scared image . . .

88

of virile man! You're not even the image of crab dung!"
Lunging at him, Matt belted me flush on the chin with an
overhand right.

I was staggered, but didn't go down. Somebody was now
laughing like a loon—*me*. "Like all idols—you're hollow!
You can't even really belt! I'm going to literally smash
your lousy image!"

Swinging wildly, I missed a left but caught him in the
belly with a solid right, took a punch on the eye which
made me think the stars had fallen. My gut **blow** doubled
Matt over; grabbing his famous hair with **my left hand**, I
yanked his head up—felt my right shatter his nose bone.
I kept punching and clubbing away until his face was a
bloody hunk of meat, mouth a mess of torn lips and broken
teeth . . . kept punching until I could no longer raise my
right—nor fight off Ruita and McCarthy pulling at me.

I let go of Matt's silvery hair . . . he crumpled to the
sand, blood all over him. Placing my arms around Ruita,
I walked her toward the dink, gasping, "Honey . . . we're
going home!"

She nodded, crying, kissing my puffed eye, then the raw
knuckles of my right hand. Looking sick, McCarthy was
kneeling over Matt.

As Ruita sat in the stern of the dink, I took the oars
and Eddie pushed us off. When he climbed in, motioned
for the oars, I told him, "If you want to stay, I'll sail the
HOOKER to Numega, you pick it up later."

Eddie and I understood each other perfectly; he knew
I wasn't being nasty—nor asking him to pass up a big
piece of change. Rowing, his brown puss broke into a
smile as he said, "You ain't much of a navigator with two
eyes, probably pile up the boat with that pip of a shiner
you got. And what's around here but a stink? I'm no body-
guard, no flunky. Hell, I've a boat and a new suit of sails
waiting. Maybe I'll return here—in about a year . . . for
trade, see how Titin looks and. . . . Hey, you think she'll
go to Hollywood?"

The Coin of Adventure

CHAPTER 1

It was the first time a well-stacked bathing suit ever made me uneasy. Not even a bikini, but an old-fashioned, long job . . . although every curve of the sultry babe filling the suit was strictly up-to-date.

Viareggio is part of one of the world's longest beaches, 26 sandy miles fronting the blue Mediterranean. It was the middle of a sunny afternoon, the sand crowded with vacationists up from Rome, plus a few English tourists.

The girl looked about 23. She and her kid brother seemed to be working for a stocky blind man who ran a stand selling fried cakes. The little boy, in ragged shorts, walked beside the girl, carrying a tray of food as they went from bather to bather. The gal's skin, naturally swarthy, was a deep golden brown from the sun, the eyes dark and flashing, lovely jet black hair hanging to compact hips.

I don't know why she reminded me of Valerie—who is blonde, her pale baby-face more cute than beautiful. Could be they had the same strong legs and trim hips in common, a sexy aura, a . . . I was afraid to think of Valerie.

It was stupid: about now Valerie would be in Paris on her see-a-100-European-cities-in-30-days tour. Instead of resting my dusty on this 'Riviera della Versilia,' as the Italian tourist ads call it, I could put my plane down in Paris within two hours, take over with Valerie where we'd left off—in an Athens hotel room.

Valerie was the best between the sheets, we had something great going . . . but she frightened me. Valerie stood for the marriage routine.

My boss' wife is Italian and her folks have a small farm inland from the Lido di Camoicre, so every time we were in Northern Italy I'd land at Pisa and he'd spend the day with his in-laws. I had been in Viareggio a dozen times before, even knew a few telephone numbers. But somehow—and I sure never believed it could happen to me—Valerie had ruined love-for-pay gals for me. At least for now.

Taking a long swim, I returned to the beach restless as before. I walked around, drying off, my knee in good shape, wondering why the Romans traveled hundreds of miles north to swim when they had a fine beach outside Rome. Or was this a status bit? And why the hell did I care?

My being restless didn't make sense. I had the ideal job air-chauffeuring the European manager of Pan-Texas Oil. We could be eating supper in Rotterdam, have breakfast in Oran, Cairo, Oslo, or Tel Aviv, the following morning. Willard Moore wasn't a demanding executive, the pay was fine, and until I'd met Valerie in Nice it had seemed a dandy job—or as perfect as any 'job' can be.

When the gal in the dark old bathing suit started hustling her cakes my way, I picked up my towel and headed toward the Hotel Marchony. It was early—Moore was to phone by 6 P.M. to let me know when he'd be at the Pisa airport.

My room was cool and after smacking a few mosquitos, I stretched out for a cat-nap. When I awoke it was 7:30 P.M. and growing dark. Dressing quickly I went down to bawl out the desk clerk. But Moore hadn't phoned. I couldn't understand that—he's the prompt type. I had supper in the hotel and at 9 P.M. told the desk clerk I'd return in an hour. I went for a walk along the Via Giosue Carducci, the main drag and promenade facing the sea.

Tourists are Viareggio's business and the street was one outdoor cafe after another, most of them sporting small bands trying their best to beat out rock and roll and making a hell of a racket, with singers sure they were Sinatra or Peggy Lee, and even one clown making with a lousy imitation of Belafonte. I had a few beers and when I returned to the Marchony there still wasn't any phone call. Hanging around for another half hour, I figured Moore was spending the night with his in-laws: all the in-law jokes to the contrary, he got along fine with his. But it was odd he hadn't phoned, or driven by in his rented Fiat.

I went for another restless walk, stopping to see what the movie was in the Principe de Piemonte, then staring out at the bobbing lights of the few fishing boats, wishing Valerie was beside me. I began walking toward the Lido di Camoicre: not because I expected to see Mr. Moore, but in that direction the promenade was quiet, free of cafes and shops.

As I was strolling along the dimly lit boardwalk, still thinking of Valerie, I saw a dozen or so Italian men, mostly teenagers, walking toward me. They weren't talking, which was strange for any group of Italians. As we passed, they turned and jumped me.

I weigh 205 pounds and have taken care of myself in plenty of ring and street brawls. I belted somebody's jaw, landed a flurry of belly punches, got my knees working—before I went down. A fist banged my nose, another brought blood to my lips, while a sharp shoe headed for my groin: hit my thigh. Curling up to protect my belt buckle, I kept twisting and kicking, trying to get punching room. Although there were so many guys on top of me I couldn't see the sky or stars, I did have a fast glimpse of a stocky guy leaping off a bike, rushing toward us. I was too busy to wonder if he was joining the pile-up. A foot caught the side of my head and I had a fight against blacking out. Then I saw this stocky guy pick up a man with his right hand, hurl him to the ground, neatly flattening another with his left.

There were Italian curses and cries of pain. I was able to roll away, jump to my feet. The old ache was in my left knee but I was too busy to worry about it. Stocky was a balding man with a crown of yellow hair, his shirt ripped and bloody, swinging like a sock machine. I was throwing wallops fast as I could, picking my spots—a stomach belt takes the fight out of most jokers.

A punch closed my right eye as I worked my way so I'd be back-to-back with my new buddy. A bus passed, the few passengers crowding the windows to stare with big eyes. The two of us were battling the wrong odds, at least 20 guys were still standing, and as I kicked a punk on his ankle, hooked another in his gut, I heard the sound

95

of running feet and knew we'd had it—a new gang of men were rushing at us!

Gasping from a solid poke under the ribs, I was startled to see the same gal I'd been watching on the beach —now wearing a white blouse and tight pants—at the head of this new gang!

The bastards slugging us also saw the newcomers and to my amazement—and relief—they took off—darting across the street and into the darkness of the side streets. The second bunch, with the gal in the lead—something dark and short in her hand, like a blackjack, raced after them . . . and soon my blonde buddy and I were alone. I fell against a railing, panting, trying to see out of my puffed eye, rubbing my bad knee.

He staggered over to lean beside me. He was in rough shape, blood gushing from his nose and big mouth, shirt in shreds, blood on his slacks. In Italian he puffed, "What happened?" I think that's what he asked—my Italian is only fair.

In English I gasped, "Thanks a million, mister. You came in the . . ."

He gave me a big grin—he had this long, lantern jaw— the light from the nearest lamp post showing puffed lips as he yelled, "Man, you from the States?"

I nodded. The belly wallop still had me sucking for air.

He stuck out his bruised right hand. "Hell of a way for two Yanks to meet! Or maybe the best way. Jimmy Johnson from Philadelphia!"

"Kent Kelly, San Diego." Shaking his hand, I saw my own knuckles were bleeding. "And again—much thanks for helping me."

"I don't stand for anybody being ganged-up. Man, this was more exciting than watching Maris and Mantle pole a couple of homers back to back! What's this all about?"

Johnson had this kind of accent, or twang, making him sound more mid-West than Philly. "Wish I knew. Guess they were trying to mug me," I said slowly, fighting for air. I felt of my pockets: had my wallet, keys, and papers. "Juvenile delinquency seems to be a world problem."

"Man, you for real? Kelly, those weren't kids, they were men! One of the punks walloped like Liston!" Jimmy Johnson said, tearing off a hunk of his shirt to wipe his sweaty face. He looked about 45, the thick, sloping shoulders made him seem short, but his blue eyes were level with mine, making him 6 feet, at least. "Who was the second gang, the Marines?" he asked, feeling his teeth with stubby fingers, finding his choppers were all there.

"Beats me. But I'm for them—whoever they are."

"I was returning my bike to a shop near the port, a rent-a-bike . . ." Johnson suddenly slapped his pockets, began looking around the boardwalk.

"They get your wallet?"

He shook his blonde-bald head. "Worse—my passport. Had it in my hip pocket. . . . It's gone!"

We both started searching in the dim light and over near the grass I finally saw the thin little green booklet. When I handed it to Johnson, he sighed with relief, opened it, showing me the usual evil-looking passport photo, of himself. "Yeah, it's mine—there's my kisser. Man, that would be rugged, losing Uncle Sam's passport. I'd best go back to my hotel, get another shirt. Too late to return the bike now, but. . . ."

"Let me buy you a shirt."

"Forget it, Kelly, I enjoyed the exercise," he said, starting for his bike. "It was a real swinger."

"Wait a minute, Johnson. I insist upon buying you a shirt and slacks. You saved me from a pasting."

"Don't worry about it, man. I've another thing cooking —a hot *signorina* waiting. You understand, have to clean up fast before I frighten the chick. See you Kelly—it's been fun!" He ran across the grass, jumped on his bike.

I started after him but my trick knee gave and I had to grab the rail. As he peddled off into the darkness I called, "Jimmy, I'm staying at the Hotel Marchony."

"Okay, Kelly."

"I'll probably check out in the morning. Call me—I insist upon buying you a shirt," I yelled, but he was gone. I saw a bench several hundred feet away; leaning against the rail I started for it. Whenever my knee gives there's nothing to do but rest the leg for a few hours. I reached the bench, wondering how the devil I'd make it back to the hotel.

This little problem was answered seconds later when a jeep braked to a roaring stop and three Italian cops—clubs in hand—jumped out. They didn't speak much English and my Italian wasn't up to explaining whatever they were after. I switched to French, which I know a little better, gathered they'd had a phone call about a riot, had come to investigate. I tried to explain I really didn't know much more than they did about the brawl, but would appreciate a lift to my hotel. After much hand gesturing and sputtering by all of us, one of the cops motioned for me to take a seat in the jeep. I never did learn if they were going to ride me to my hotel or to the local jail—my knee folded again and they carried me to the jeep.

Driving as if I was an emergency case, they rushed to the Viareggio hospital. A doctor and two nurses examined me. There was more hand-waving and talk in bad Italian, French and English as I insisted there wasn't a thing wrong with me a piece of raw steak wouldn't cure. They kept touching my knee, filling it with pain. I gave up attempting to explain it was just an old football injury. I had this horrible hunch they were getting ready to operate, was wondering if I'd have to punch my way out of the curiously barren hospital . . . when a young doctor sporting a snappy red beard entered the room, asked in crisp English, "What seems to be the trouble, *signore?*"

"No trouble, Doc—I merely have a black eye. Look, can you call a cab for me, let me return to my hotel?"

He studied my face with sad eyes. "Ah yes, you indeed have a discolored eye. And your leg, they say you can not walk."

"A bad tackle did that years ago. All my leg needs is a good night's rest."

One of the policemen rattled off some fast Italian and red beard nodded, asked me, "Exactly what happened to you, *signore?*"

"Doc, I was out for a walk when I was suddenly jumped by a gang of young men—about 25 of them. Happily another American came by, saved me from a bad beating. I mean, well, a second bunch of men—and a girl—they came along and chased the first gang. It's all confusing."

"Yes, it is," he said slowly, stroking his trim red beard, "Were you robbed?"

"They didn't have a chance to take me."

"Are you carrying anything of value, *signore?*"

98

"Well—no. Credit cards and travelers' checks, but only about $30 in francs and lira."

"Not much of a prize for—25 men, I believe you said, to fight over. This other . . . eh . . . gang, with a girl. . . . ?"

"A beautiful babe," I cut in.

"Ah yes, a beautiful girl," the doctor said, blinking. "Did the second gang identify themselves, say anything?"

"Not that I could understand."

"You seem sober, so it turns out to be quite a ruddy puzzle. First, considering you were attacked by 25 men, even though you and this other American chap were able to fight off such odds, it is amazing you have but a few minor bruises. Also, we rarely have crimes of a gang nature—in Italy."

I knew he was digging me, had seen too many of Hollywood's gangster movies, but I was too bushed for an argument—merely wanted to get back to my hotel and my bed.

The cop asked something in Italian and red beard asked me in his 'English' English, "Sir, are you involved in politics?"

"Me? Hell no!"

"Are you in Italy as a tourist?"

"My name is Kent Kelly and I'm a pilot for Pan-Texas Oil. I'm staying at the Hotel Marchony. I flew in around noon at Pisa . . ."

Red beard's sad face suddenly lit up. "Ah, this is a blooming piece of fine luck, Mr. Kelly. I have been trying to phone you for the past hour. Your employer is here."

"Mr. Moore . . . Willard Moore . . . here?"

"He was in an auto accident this afternoon, suffered fractured ribs and minor facial injuries. Although for a time I thought he had a concussion and. . . ."

"Can I see him?"

"Of course, *Signore* Moore has been asking for you. Come with me."

I followed the little doctor into a small, private room, to see my boss in bed, bandaged like a mummy. Only his eyes, the lower part of his face, and one shoulder, were free of bandages and/or tape. His thin nose was so swollen he looked comical.

Smiling up at me, Moore waved a bandaged hand and

asked, "What hit you, Kent? Seems to have been a rough day for Pan-Texas employees."

"I was on the wrong end of a mob scene. But what about this accident you were in, Mr. Moore?" I always have a hard time trying to decide whether to call him 'Mister' or not. I don't like saying 'mister' or 'sir,' but at the same time if you get too friendly with an employer you leave yourself wide open, don't know where you stand.

"I was side-swiped by a truck, hit a soft shoulder on the road, and the Fiat turned over."

"I was waiting for your call and . . ." I turned to red beard. "If this happened in the afternoon, why didn't the hospital phone me sooner?"

"*Signore* Moore was in a state of shock, placed under sedation. He only awoke a short time ago."

Moore told me, "Kent, call the London office and explain that I'll be laid up here for at least a week."

"Yes sir."

"Also see about the damage to the car—an insurance policy was part of the rental fee. Let London know the cost, and the rest of the details, after you talk to the rental office in Pisa. I think we have lawyers in Rome, or Milan, if it comes to that."

"I'll attend to it, be back tomorrow afternoon. Do you need cigarettes, books?"

"I'm quite comfortable and it won't be necessary for you to return here, Kent. No point in you hanging around Viareggio—take the week off, fly to see that nurse you met in Athens." Moore gave me a hammy wink. "Do what you wish but be at the Pisa airport next Tuesday morning."

"I'll probably stay around Viareggio, I have some things to do."

"Suit yourself, but keep out of brawls—this is a small hospital. By the way, this mob you said attacked you, did any one of them have a scar on his right cheek? Sharp-nosed man with an old scar in the shape of a ragged half-moon?"

"There wasn't much light and the action came down too fast to make out faces. What's with the scar bit, Mr. Moore?"

"I had a flash-look at the driver of the truck. He wore

an floppy old hat, but I did see the scar on his cheek, his nose."

Red beard said, *"Signore* Moore believes his accident was deliberate. I have told this to the police—they disagree. Neither the accident nor a damaged truck have been reported, so far. As for a scar . . ." The doctor rubbed his red beard. "Italy has been ravaged by two great wars, there are thousands of men with scars and other bloody marks of violence."

My boss waved a bandaged hand. "I can't prove it was deliberate, certainly no reason for anybody to want me dead or crippled. But the fact remains the road was empty ——I always take this back road out of Viareggio, brings me right to the farm——there was ample room for this old truck to pass me. You know what a cautious driver I am, Kent."

"You crawl along, Mr. Moore. This scar-face, was he old or young? What about his size, the color of his hair?"

"Look, I only had a split-second glimpse of a sharp face dominated by this old scar."

"The truck, what did that look like?"

Moore tried to shrug and his eyes clouded with pain. "Very old and heavy. I don't know. . . . Perhaps it was an accident. In any event I'll be here for the next three or four days, then I'll spend a day or two with my in-laws. I've already cabled my wife to stay in Sweden, no point of her rushing down here. You do what you wish, but be in Pisa by Tuesday. I have an important appointment in Morocco Tuesday afternoon . . . at 4 P.M." Moore's voice sounded tired and he closed his eyes.

Red beard motioned for me to follow him into the hallway, where he asked, "I meant to ask, did you recognize any of the men you claim attacked you? Or the girl?"

"What do you mean I 'claim' attacked me!" I pointed to my puffed eye. "You think I clouted myself?"

"Merely a figure of speech, perhaps my English is not right," he said, sarcastically. "Did you know any of the . . . eh . . . gang?"

"No." I wasn't going to let the police grab the gal peddling fried cakes on the beach——I had other things in mind for her. "Forget about my trouble; isn't it funny the truck driver *didn't* report Moore's accident?"

101

"Funny?" A puzzled frown swept the doctor's delicate face. "Ah yes, I understand—you do not mean the ha-ha funny, but the strange, the odd, funny."

"Look, ha-ha or ho-hum, don't all traffic accident *have* to be reported here?"

"Let us say they bloody well should be reported, and generally are. *Signore* Kelly, my county has some of the world's best educated people, and plenty of illiterates. Unhappily it has always been thus. A farmer may have been too blasted frightened to report the accident. The more serious the accident, the greater his fright—and silence. Happily *Signore* Moore's injuries are minor. Come, I will put some salve on your eye—by morning the swelling and coloring should be back to normal."

When the police jeep finally dropped me off at the Marchony, I was certain some of the plump Roman tourists gassing in the lobby made snide cracks about "drunken Americans." But I was too beat to think of anything except a fast shower and lots of shut-eye. Even a tight formation of mosquitos buzzing my face didn't stop me from falling off into a deep sleep.

CHAPTER 2

I awoke before 8 A.M. feeling great, my knee working okay and the black eye barely noticeable against my tan. I considered going for a swim, settled for a cold shower. I wanted to see the babe selling cakes on the beach . . . closing my eyes I pictured her as she'd been last night, the neat way she held the blackjack. She was my kind of babe.

But last night was merely a daydream, my immediate problem was—should I fly to Paris, take Valerie off that silly-ass tour and into the nearest bed? I had to admit I

102

wanted her far more than I ever thought I'd desire any girl. But the thought of hurting Valerie—having her cry would be the messy end of something which had been really beautiful. True, I had a week off, but considering what about 12 hours with Valerie had done to me, seven days with her would be damn risky.

The way things broke in less than two hours I would forget Valerie—but of course I didn't know that as I went down stairs, put away lots of eggs and orange juice, cups of frothy coffee expresso. I thought of facing Valerie across a breakfast table for the rest of my life—and almost bought the deal.

After the desk clerk phoned to learn when the auto-for-hire office in Pisa opened, I returned to my room to shave. The maid had already made up the room, the Marchony is a very efficient hotel. I was still debating whether to pack a bag, fly from Pisa to Paris. Taking out a large Swiss coin —my pocket was like an international bank—I tossed to see if I'd risk going to Valerie. Heads I'd fly to her.

The coin landed on the dresser top, heads up. My better judgment warned me this was far too important for heads/tails—that was kid stuff. In fact better judgment shouted to forget Valerie or I'd end up hooked for life.

I walked to the corner and caught the Pisa bus. Some 20 minutes later I was the only passenger who didn't get off at the Leaning Tower stop, but went on to the center of town. It was going to be another hot day and I hoped to hell somebody in the car office spoke English, so I could be on the beach before noon. Or would I be in Paris by then?

Crossing the street to the auto shop I heard a man shout, "Hey, Kelly!"

My blond buddy of last night rushed toward me, small packages in his arms. Johnson was wearing a loud Hawaiian sport shirt, pale blue slacks, and moccasin casuals. In the daylight he was a tough-looking oscar, thick muscled and lean, big face having a rugged ugliness. I bet with his blue eyes the gals thought him handsome. The remains of his yellow hair were salted with grey and I figured he was reaching fifty, certainly in top shape. His upper lip was still swollen, there was a bruise on his thick neck.

Pumping my hand he said, "Man, I was going to drop

in to see you this afternoon. Came to Pisa to buy a few crappy souvenirs for the folks back home. You been up to the Tower yet?"

"I'm here on business, my boss' car was smashed. Come in with me, and then I'll buy you a drink. After last night I owe you a bottle—at least."

"Wasn't that something? Best fight since Gordie Howe mixed with Lou Fontinato in the Garden, back in February '59."

"What weight do they fight?"

Jimmy Johnson gave me a sly look. "They ain't pugs. Hockey, man! Howe was with the Detroit Red Wings and Fontinato played on the New York Rangers. They put on a riot."

"Yeah? I rarely see hockey," I said, as we entered the car-rental shop. Several of the clerks spoke English and everybody seemed embarrassed by the accident. Pan-Texas obviously was a bigger customer than I knew. I was assured the insurance covered the wreck—and the Fiat was a total wreck—plus they had some claim papers for Moore to fill out; he might collect up to a million lire for his injuries. I asked if they had heard anything about the truck which hit Moore and was told they hadn't—it didn't make any difference, the insurance still covered everything.

I gave them the address of the hospital, had a clerk help me phone the London office—collect—and explained to a bored English voice about Moore being out for a week. I finished with a little brown-nosing, had the clerk phone the Viareggio hospital. Moore was sleeping but I left a message that I'd called, the insurance claims were on the way.

Johnson said all he wanted to drink was a beer and we had a couple under the awning of a sidewalk cafe near the bus terminal. I was still tossing my mind about: should I fly to Paris or return to Viareggio?

Jimmy Johnson said, "I couldn't help but overhear, you have a week off with pay. What kind of jobs are there over here, for Americans?"

"Very few. I've been over for nearly ten months, but my pay comes from the States. I'm a private pilot for an

104

American oil company executive. My boss was riding from the airport when . . ."

"Oh Lord, *you're a pilot?*" Johnson cut in, hard face stupid with disbelief, lantern chin almost touching the table.

"Sure. I hop all over Europe, North Africa."

"You mean you've been here, in Pisa, before, Kelly?"

"At least a dozen times. Why?"

Johnson took a fast gulp of his beer. "Great Gordon Gin, that we two should meet——makes me believe in Fate and all that mystic jazz! Kelly, you interested in taking a crack at a million bucks, maybe more, in the next few days?"

It was my turn to stare like an open-mouth idiot. "What crazy words your big flabby mouth makes! Jimmy, who are you?"

"Me? Back in Philly I'm a postal worker. Listen, does Dongo mean anything to you?" His voice slid to a whisper.

Before I could ask if he was talking about another hockey player, Johnson shook his bald dome, added, "No, you weren't old enough to have been in World War Two."

"I was too damn young even for Korea," I said bitterly really talking to myself.

Johnson glanced around the cafe, bent over the table as he said in a low voice, "Italy's trouble has always been a lack of natural resources, but there is wealth here which hasn't been tapped——yet! Dongo is a village on a lake north of Milano and there's supposed to be a hundred million bucks in that lake!"

"Oil?" I whispered, wondering if Jimmy was a nut——he didn't look like an oil man. Nor like a post office clerk—— unless he worked out daily with bar bells.

Johnson chuckled, whispered in his Kansas-like twang, "No man, I'm talking about gold, jewels . . . loot! A hundred cases dumped there by Mussolini as he was trying to reach Switzerland, and then on to South America. The windbag never made it, was killed by a band of partisans. But while they were chasing his convoy he's supposed to have dumped his loot chests into the lake at Dongo. Kesselring, who commanded the German forces in Italy, is said to have abandoned some five million bucks in jewels and art works in a cave near Verona. The Desert Fox, Rom-

105

mel, packed half a dozen great caskets full of swag from Africa. He got them far as Corsica, where an SS officer named Fleig was supposed to bring them by boat to La Spezia. The chests weighed so much they nearly capsized the boat in rough seas, so Fleig is said to have dumped them in a hundred feet of water, off the village of Bastia, on Corsica. There are reports of other hidden treasures— from the family silver small-fry Blackshirt officials buried in their back yards before following the Nazi army into Germany—to the tale of a plane flying gold from Hitler to Mussolini, which crashed some place in the Alps—never been found. Despite what the military experts write in their technical books, the real reason for war is always loot— in one form or another."

My guts began to glow with excitement. "All this on the level, Jimmy?"

"Hard to say for sure. I've read every article I could find on this. In fact, it was a piece about the Dongo hoard a couple years ago which got me interested in. . . ."

"But an article can be so many gassy words? The war ended almost . . . 18 years ago: if the loot really was there, wouldn't it have been found by now?"

Johnson shrugged thick shoulders. "True, the stories probably are exaggerated, but also they must be based on *some* facts. Okay, perhaps there's only a million or two— instead of a hundred million—buried. In the course of my reading I learned Fleig, the SS man who dumped Rommel's loot, is alive, trying to raise money to go after 'his' treasure. There's supposed to have been two Nazi officers with Mussolini and they're still alive—some years ago they offered to show the Italian government where the hundred cases were—in exchange for a cut. The Italians said no dice, according to the article. Also a rumor some of the partisans were Communists, used the treasure to finance the Italian Red party. But forget rumors, the other treasure stories— I'm only interested in the Dongo loot. Are you?"

"I'm still ears! I've done some skin-diving, Jimmy, and . . ."

"Damnit, keep your voice down, Kelly!" Johnson cut in, glancing at the other cafe tables. The few customers weren't paying us any mind. "Listen to me again, Kelly. Mussolini's convoy of motor cars started for the Swiss border at night. They were being followed by the 'party-johns,' as the partisans were called, so the convoy was in a hell of a hurry. Even a small casket of gold and jewels is heavy. How far into the lake could men running for their lives have tossed a box weighing at least three or four hundred pounds? Hell, even if they weren't on the run, how far could they toss a heavy trunk?"

"Not more than 10 feet. If articles have been written about this and it's not more than a dozen feet from shore, there's something cockeyed, if it hasn't been found during all these years!"

Johnson nodded, gave me a puffed-lip grin. "Exactly what I thought! So it adds up to this—the story is a lot of crap, the cases were *never* thrown into the lake! All of Mussolini's party were gunned down, except those two Nazi officers who escaped. But they would have returned for the loot if it was that simple to find!"

"Johnson, what the hell you doing, turning me on? If it's all a lot of gas, where does that leave us?"

For a split second his face turned mean with suspicion, the long jaw tight. Then he smiled and whispered, "Kelly, you're not as sharp as I thought. Last night, and now—ordering these beers—you didn't notice I speak good Italian. I was an orphan, raised by Italian foster parents on a chicken farm outside Philly. I grew up speaking Italian and when I was drafted, the army put me into the OSS, sent me to Italy—behind the lines north of Rome. Not only because I spoke the lingo, my foster folks had relatives around Milan. Most of the time I was on my own, working with partisan units and . . ."

"Were you in on the killing of Mussolini?"

"Not exactly. Listen to me, carefully. In 1945 when Musso was captured and strung up by his fat heels, the was was about over on the Italian front, with the super-race, the Nazis, on the run. Well, I was goofing off—told you I was on my own most of the time. I was shacking up with an Eye-tie broad not far from Dungo, the same night Musso was captured. Okay, I'm not in the woods, under a blanket with this girl, my mind far from war, when a small blast ripped the night some miles away. Being an OSS man, trained in guerrilla fighting, I recognized it as a dynamite charge. I wondered what the hell it was all about

——but only vaguely, I was shaking the earth in my own little way at the time. Remember. . . ."

"Stop the corn and come to the point."

"Trying to, Kelly, so shut up. Remember, dynamite is hard to buy in a poor country, impossible to get during war time. I knew the partisans didn't have much of the stuff and my intelligence reports didn't have any partisan units operating in the area. I forgot about it, figured I'd made a mistake, either somebody had stepped on a land mine or a drunk found a grenade, pulled the ring. Kelly, is the picture coming into focus?"

"No. What did you do about the blast you heard?"

"Keep your voice down!" Johnson's big kisser suddenly relaxed, he showed his strong teeth in another grin. "I did nothing, sat on the bench, didn't bother to take a cut at the ball. Remember, I was busy making love, the war was about over here, so an isolated blast wasn't of any importance. But——" He held up his lumpy right hand like a ham actor——"about a dozen years later, when I first read of this Dongo treasure, I began wondering why the loot hadn't been found if it was merely dumped in a few feet of water. Skin-diving is popular here in Italy, too. The rest of the story is simple——recalling that odd dynamite blast I figured *Musso never had the loot dumped in the lake, but stashed it in some cave, then dynamited the entrance to close it! The bull about tossing the trunks into the lake was strictly a cover-up, to safeguard the real spot——the cave!*"

"Italian hills and mountains are full of caves," I said, losing some of my excitement.

"I have a good idea where it is. The morning after the blast, I scouted around, merely out of curiosity, found evidence of a blast on a hillside. Of course, at the time it didn't mean a thing to me. But ever since I started reading these articles, I've had nothing on my mind except taking a crack at finding the treasure. This is why I came to Italy a week ago. I've a month's vacation and . . ."

"Did you find the cave?"

"Yeah——I found the spot. I also ran up against a big hurdle, which is why I'm cutting you in——the Italian government will never allow me to take the loot from the country, or keep it. I figured the big seaports would be

108

too risky, so I've been asking around Viareggio for a boat large enough to take me to France. But I don't know anybody, haven't much money, and naturally it's dangerous to talk about what I have in mind. But you, man, you're my answer! Customs men will never question or stop your oil company plane—it will all seem like one of your routine flights. We hop to Paris and once out of Italy —it's *all* ours!

"How much do you think is there?"

"Don't be greedy, Kelly. Keep in mind we're playing an 'iffy' long shot. There might be too much digging for us— we'll have to work fast and secretly, at night. Also, my entire theory can be wrong—there might not be any treasure at all, or perhaps it was done by some fleeing Italian official burying the family silver—worth a hundred bucks. But if I'm right, and even if only a few of the treasure caskets are there, splitting it 50-50, I figure we each ought to rack up a score of a million bucks, maybe five or six times a million—each! Buying it, Kelly?"

I gulped my beer to hide my excitement, damn glad I hadn't fobbed-up, gone off to see Valerie. This was the bit a guy named Kent Kelly was born for! I asked, "What's our next step, partner?"

Johnson threw back his bald head and laughed, underslung chin aimed at me. "Second I saw you, I knew you had a taste for adventure, like me!" His voice dropped to a harsh whisper. "Our first step is to keep our traps shut! I can't stress this too much, Kelly. Let the Italian officials even smell what we're up to and they'll tail us, take the treasure, boot our cans out of the country—if they don't throw us under the jail. Our best bet is to act like a couple of hick American tourists. Anybody asks, at your hotel, you're going sight-seeing. We'll need a car. Can you rent one here, on the oil company's account?"

"I could but I won't—pay for it myself. When do we start?"

"Get the car, the usual small Fiat station wagon tourists hire. Tell 'em you plan a camping trip to Rome, or Bari. We'll return to Viareggio, it's on our way north, and I have some tools at my place. If we leave by noon we can be in Milan at 6 P.M., at the cave by nine."

"I only have a week off," I said, realizing how dumb I

109

sounded—with a million in sight I was worrying about my flying-chauffeur job. Still, as Johnson said, all we might end up with was a pain in the back from digging.

"Man, if things move for us, we should be in France this time tomorrow, with enough folding money to last a lifetime! Let's get off the dime, Kelly old boy!"

Within a half hour I was driving a midget station wagon to Viareggio, Johnson talking baseball all the way. He was one of these nutty fans who memorize a record book. Did I know Whitey Ford's pitching arm was two inches longer than his right hand, from all his years of pitching? Had I seen Al Gionfriddo's impossible catch of DiMiggio's homer, practically in the Dodger bullpen, with Stirnwess and Yogi Berra crossing home plate, the mighty Joe rounding second, as Gionfriddo fell down but still held on to the ball?

I couldn't have cared less, my little brain was working like an adding machine. Hell, with his million buck cut Johnson could buy his own ball team. Me, I was dreaming of a villa along the Riviera, or cruising the South Seas.

Reaching my hotel, I said I'd pack in a few seconds, then drive Jimmy to where he was staying, but he suggested I lend him the car—he'd return by noon. He wanted to buy a few crowbars and two Yanks shopping for such a non-tourist item might look suspicious. I didn't like the idea of giving up the car . . . had a flash of caution: was he pulling some kind of con game on me? But then I felt like a jerk—I'd seen his passport, Jimmy was okay. He was cutting me in on a million and I was worried about a rented car.

He drove off and I went up to my room, started to pack a small bag. I wondered if I'd ever return to the hotel, should I take all my clothes with me? I decided not to check out of the Marchony. Pan-Texas was footing the bill. I travel light, if we hit it, what the devil was a few suits? If it turned out we were on a fool's errand, I'd return as if nothing had happened.

Having time to kill, I put on my trunks and went out to the beach—to see the gal who reminded me of Valerie, ask about last night. I had no trouble finding her, almost had a feeling she was waiting for me.

Filling the same old worn swim suit so well, the minute

I stepped on the sand she left her kid brother with his tray of fried cakes, came over and said, "Hello. I was hoping to see you."

"Two minds with a single thought. You speak English well. My name is Kelly—Kent Kelly."

"I teach English in our school. I am Marisa." She pointed toward the shade of the bathhouse porch. "We sit and talk, if you do not mind." Her voice was throaty and everything about her—the feathery dark eyebrows, even the sweat of her hot body, had a sensuous sound, look, and smell: shouted sex. Yet I kept thinking about Valerie— didn't know why Marisa reminded me of Valerie. On the surface, with her cute face, you'd never suspect what an explosion Valerie could be in bed. But one look at Marisa and you knew she *had* to be all heat.

I motioned for the attendant to bring canvas chairs, place them on the shady side of the porch, tossed a couple 100 lire bills his way. I asked Marisa if she wanted a cigarette but she shook her head impatiently—so many things shaking beside the long black hair. She asked, "Why did the fascists attack you last night?"

"Fascists? They were a gang of muggers."

A frown crossed the warm features. "What means . . . muggers?"

"Thieves—small time punks."

Marisa shook her head again, and what wonderful breasts she had. "Oh no. No. They were neo-fascists. I belong to the Left Democrats and we keep an eye on these fools. It is rare they have courage to attack in the open. One of our men saw them gathering near beach last night, I immediately rounded-up members of our party, came to see what was going on. You are in politics in the United States, *Signore* Kelly?"

"Kent's the name, honey. Politics—I don't even know how to spell the word. Hospital doc asked me the same question. No politics in this, they were either out to rob me, or mistook me for somebody else. I thought fascism died when they strung up Benito and his mistress?"

Marisa smiled, thick lips a delicious red against the white of her even teeth. "Unfortunately no. Things do not end so simply—not even nightmares. There are frustrated youngsters and ex-Blackshirts who still dream of Italy con-

111

quering the world—the same old stupid, and impossible, sales talk Mussolini sold. Their movement is not large, but well financed, of course, and always dangerous. They are strongest in Rome, Venice, and here—wherever the wealthy gather. You look so—so American, it is difficult to think they mistook you for somebody else."

"It was pretty dark. Did you catch any of them?"

"No, we did not wish to, only to see what they were doing. When we saw them beating you two, we ran for them, of course. Have you been in Italy long, Kent? What a wonderful name, Kent Kelly, like a *feelm* star. You even look like *Americano feelm* star, tall and strong with nice wave in hair."

I found myself actually blushing at her bold stare. "You could pass for a starlet yourself, Marisa honey. I fly for a U.S. oil company, plane all over Europe. I've been in Italy a lot of times, but only for a day or so each time. Marisa, you're off on the wrong track, when it comes to politics I don't know which end is up. Back in the States, I've never even voted."

She kept staring at me, dark eyes all passion, then she laughed and it felt like a caress. "You are what they call in your slang, a real live doll, Kent."

It was such an unexpected crack, and the comical way she pronounced it, made me laugh. "Marisa, you and I have to see lots more of each other."

"I would like that."

"Look, I . . . eh . . . have to leave Viareggio today, on business, but I'll be back in a few days and then we'll really ball, honey."

"You can always find me on the beach, we have concession. Where you go on business?"

"Genoa, then over to Nice," I said, lying smoothly, amused at her clumsy cross-examination. "Like to take a swim?"

"I am not much of a swimmer."

"Fine, I'll teach you." I corned, jumping to my feet, hiding my cigarettes in the sand under the chair.

Marisa got to her feet, sailed her black hair into a turban. With her hands to her head each graceful movement seemed an invitation, even the cluster of damp dark hair under her armpits sent my temperature into orbit. I took

112

her hand and we crossed the hot sand to the water, Marisa calling out something in Italian to her kid brother who grinned at us, waved his tray of cakes. The kid went over to the blind man, cooking the cakes at his stand, said a few words, pointed his skinny arm at us. The blind man turned his head so he faced the sea, nodded. I wondered how Marisa's father had become blind.

Wading out until the salt water was up to my chest, and her chin, I showed off—swimming under water to pinch her neat thighs, standing on my hands. Marisa couldn't swim at all but didn't seem nervous as she jumped up and down to ride each wave.

I conned her out farther, over her head. She put her hands around my neck while my mitts were on her firm waist, lifting her over the wave tops, brushing her wonderful bosom against my chest. She calmly held on to me, the warm eyes studying my face and judging by the smile her lush lips formed, finding me okay. Her direct way of looking at me was embarrassing. I said, "Long as you stay relaxed, you'll never drown. Tenseness somehow destroys human buoyancy. Did you know that bit of wisdom, Marisa?" I knew I was talking like a jerk.

"No. But I am relaxed, not afraid. For the first years of my life my favorite rattle was an empty hand grenade and I slept at my mother's breast to din of bomb blasts, the firing of cannon. I am . . . how you say . . . a true child of war, and such a child does not live if she is afraid. Also, you live doll, stop rubbing me against you."

I laughed, delighted with her frankness. Marisa had *my* feeling for adventure, living dangerously. I told her, "It's the sea pushing you against me."

"Then remember the sea is very strong, needs no help. Does your company sell oil for military use?"

"I don't know, honey. I guess we sell it any place we can make a buck. What makes you ask?"

"I am still puzzled as why they singled you out for attack last night."

"Keep telling you, they thought I was carrying a fat green bundle. Forget them and . . ."

"Fat green bundle? Of what?" Marisa asked sharply, spitting salt water.

"Money. They thought I was loaded with dollars."

113

"No, they are stupid and vain, cruel as animals, but they are not outright thieves, surely not as a gang. And they do not lack lire or . . ."

"Forget 'em. Let me show you how to swim. Simply lie on your belly, like this," I said, laying her on the water— my fingers working up along the smooth stomach curve to her breasts, "and move your hands as if you were cupping the water. At the same time, kick your feet."

"Like so?" Marisa asked, giving me a kick on my bum knee. She saw me wince, asked, "Did I hurt you, Kent? I only meant for you to stop being such a doll."

"I'm okay. Since you live on the beach, I'm surprised you haven't learned to swim."

"Because I must work, have little time for play. I have lost too much time from work as is. Please take me ashore."

"Sure. But you know the saying about all work and no play."

"It is not a phrase which has meaning in a poor country, like my Italy."

"Not so poor. Back in the States I read an article that this part of Italy is full of hidden treasure," I said, playing it coy, as I carried her in until she could stand. "It said the Nazi generals, Mussolini, hid their war loot in lakes."

"I have heard the murdering swine did that, but not around Viareggio—more north and at the base of the Alps. They were fleeing with their blood money and secret documents."

"But since that was almost 20 years ago, hasn't any of the loot been found?"

Marisa shrugged. "No. There was newspaper talk some years past of an SS brute and a Luftwaffe man, who had been Mussolini's bodyguards, offering to show the Italian government where some treasure was, in return for a part of it. Of course, the government could not deal with war criminals. And if anybody did stumble on such treasure, they would hardly shout about it."

"Imagine some joker diving into a lake, bumping his noggin on a million bucks!"

"Treasure is a fool's dream; work is what keeps me alive."

As we came ashore she loosened her hair, fluffed it in the strong sun. "What did your employers say of the attack on you?"

"Honey, I never told them. Pan-Texas has more to worry about than a black eye of one of its pilots."

"What do they worry about, Kent?"

"Just an expression. Guess they don't worry at all, business is A-okay." I motioned for her kid brother, took two cakes from his tray, gave one to Marisa. When I dug into the pocket of my trunks for change, she held my hand.

The cakes were pastry-crisp and as we ate I told her, "Remember, I'll be back in two days, then we'll really do the town."

"Good. You know where to find me. It is time I give my Rinaldo a rest. *Ciaou*, Kent."

I watched her walk over to take the tray from the kid, send him back to the blind man sweating over his cooking. It was amazing the blind man could cook without burning himself. I kept my eyes on the sway of Marisa's hips until she was lost among the other bathers, then returned to my beach chair, dug up my cigarettes. Lighting a butt, I walked about, drying off. I sure was going to return for Marisa: she and her kid brother were lucky to make more than a thousand lire a day—two bucks. With my cut of the loot I'd set her family up, then we'd take off— for any place in the world we wanted to see.

Taking my towel I headed for the hotel, walking slowly so as not to kick my knee out again. Marisa knew how to live. . . . Now if I told Valerie I'd come into a million bucks, she'd probably want me to invest in some lousy business. Valerie was a damn fine girl, but she had no sense of adventure, the feeling for excitement. . . .

I'd first seen her in Nice, getting off one of those tourist group buses rushing people from city to city so they could brag—back in the States—of having 'seen Europe.' Spending an hour in this city, an exhausted night in the next, they really saw nothing—merely went through the motions. I'd been crossing from the park in front of the Hotel Plaza when Valerie stepped out of the bus. I suppose I would have noticed her anyway, she was the only blonde and only young person among the tired tourists,

115

but what made me stare was—under the crumpled dress I saw the outline of her panties making a rousing V over her good hips.

Our eyes had met and then she vanished into the hotel lobby. Four days later I was amazed to see her sitting—alone—at a sidewalk cafe in Athens. Our eyes met again and I knew she remembered me. It turned out her tour had a 'free' afternoon and I wasn't leaving Athens until morning. We swam, danced, and ended up in my hotel room. In the middle of the night Valerie shook me awake, the moonlight coming through the window to make her a pale blonde goddess sitting in my bed.

"Kent, when will I see you back in the States?"

Waking, seeing this dream, I wasn't thinking of the States. I pulled her to me and later when we were searching the bed for a cool spot—pleasantly exhausted, Valerie and I were most compatible in the hay—she had asked again, "Kent, when will you return to the States?"

"Oh—that's hard to say," I'd said, hating to spoil my mood, knowing damn well what she meant, just as I knew Valerie wasn't the type who slept around.

"Is this the end of things—for us?"

I'd reached over to play with her golden hair, pinched the cute pug nose, the delicate pink nipples. "Why don't you stay in Europe with me?"

"But I have my nurse's civil service job, back home?"

"As the man says, home is where you hang your head. Toss your job over, I make enough to keep us both. Always get another job as a nurse, any time you want."

The blue eyes had really twinkled, "Are you proposing, fly-boy?"

"Valerie, honey, don't play it cute. I like you—a great deal, perhaps as much as I can like anybody, but hon—don't put the bit on the you-slept-with-me-marry-me level."

She'd said coldly, "I'd smack you, except that would be as cliché as your asinine words. Certainly I'm in bed because I want to be with you. Perhaps I'm being naive, I'm not experienced in . . . but from the way we . . . went at . . . things, it must be more than mere sex between us. I nearly went out of my mind with joy . . ."

"We hit the heights, we exploded, honey."

116

"Oh Kent, we have this . . . thing between us, if we can see each other, see how we make out in other ways . . . I'd like to marry you. I don't mean in Europe, with you jumping around like homeless rabbit. Dearest, I'm sure you can find a job in the States."

"You're so right. Hon, any time I say the word there's a slot as an airline co-pilot awaiting me. A buddy I knew in flying school is a wheel with one of the major lines. That what you want, Valerie, one of those split-level homes within driving distance of an airfield, like in Kew Gardens, with you working until the kids come, then I'll fly a regular schedule, come down at Idlewild once or twice a week, rush home to watch TV, fix the screens, mow the lawn, show our neighbors what a bang-up dry martini I can toss together? You want that, baby?"

"Yes! Oh darling I'd like that! Kent, Kent, can we have it?"

"The house is always a little more than we can afford, there will be other things straining the budget, car, school for the kids, repairs on the oil burner, but on a pilot's salary we could make it."

"Kent, we'd manage very well! I have some money in the bank and . . . Darling, it's wonderful! I don't want a big family—we'll be able to travel on your vacation . . ."

"Sure, my two week's vacation!"

Valerie had thrown herself on top of me, kissed my lips hard. "Oh Kent, what a wonderful life we'll have!"

"We could do it, but it stinks, a dull routine! I'd go nuts."

Valerie had pulled away as if I'd turned into a rattler. After a long moment she'd asked, voice cool again, "I must be a trifle dumb, but what stinks about it, as you so splendidly put it?"

"It means we've given up, tossed the towel in for the rest of our lives."

"Given up what, Kent? Would my waiting around some hotel room in Rome or Paris for you to fly in once a month, or trailing you around Europe, living out of a suitcase— would that be less dull, less of a routine? Would that be exciting living it up?"

I'd reached for her lips; Valerie had twisted away. So I'd held both her slim hands in my left, then casually placed

117

my right hand over her breast, holding her firmly—roughly, "Valerie, don't dig me because I don't know if I'd want that, either," I had told her, speaking slowly, trying to pick the right words. "Hon, if you'll forgive another spanking cliché—I'm not ready to settle down."

"You're about—26, what's bugging you, Kent?"

"Nothing: maybe everything. Take my name, when your handle is Kent Kelly, you're born for action, adventure. When . . ."

"It's a lovely name, Kent Kelly. I like the ring of it."

"It's a fighting name, hon! When I was a kid there would always be somebody saying, 'Kent Kelly—you must go for tough.' Then I'd have to lick 'em, prove myself. Perhaps all that gave me the idea I was made for adventure, shaped my plans and dreams. But the truth is, I've missed out all down the damn line—so far! I was too young for Korea, measles floored me the night I reached the Golden Glove finals, my knee went out in my first season of varsity football. Even flying becomes merely a routine job. Valerie, don't you see, once I settle down, it's an admission I've had it, that I'm done!"

"I don't mind your hand being a bra, but not now. Let go of me!"

"I'll think about it."

"Oh Kent, you don't sound well. As they say, what's in a name? Would you feel different if you changed your name to Moe Jones?"

"Clever, clever—very funny!" I snapped, taking my hand off her soft breast.

"I'm not clever, and I certainly don't feel in a humorous mood. Kent, I don't understand, just what is it you would have 'had?' Exactly what the devil is 'adventure,' fly-boy?"

"It isn't something you can fence in with words. I want . . . top excitement, real action. I want to be a . . . a . . . freebooter. I'd fly guns to Cuba, Africa, for either side! I'd . . ."

"Either side?"

"That's right, I'd do it for the sheer excitement. But the day of the soldier of fortune is over, now entire governments have become gun-runners. Honey, I don't know what I'm seeking, but I do know damn well I'm not ready to spend my nights playing bridge, gassing over some back-

118

yard fence about the next power move in PTA politics."

"Moe . . . you sound immature."

"Why? Because my ideas of living don't jibe with yours?"

"Because you talk of pirates in a jet age. Because you don't know there can be excitement in true happiness, the adventure of having each other, discovery in raising a family, action in all the daily little battles you're afraid to face!"

"Sorry, Valerie, but I'm not ready to settle for that."

"Settle? Lord I look forward to. . . . ! Well, I suppose I should at least say thanks for telling me, playing all cards face up, Moe . . . Kent. How I wish you were Moe Jones!"

There had been the pain of such downright despair in her voice I'd crushed her in my arms. Valerie held me tightly as I had whispered "Hon, I'm being honest, leveling with you. Any relationship must be built on what we really think. Sure, we can marry and maybe hit it fine—to be honest and above the belt again. Frankly, in my own way I'm kind of nuts about you, never had a girl turn me on like you do. I don't know, maybe this is the real business for us, maybe I love you. Listen, Valerie, give me time. I'd be no good to you the way I am—full of wild hairs. Perhaps in a year or so, I'll have found whatever I want, or think I want, be ready for your kind of living. Will you do that, for me? Understand, I'm not asking you to wait, but don't . . . slam the door, lock me out, either."

"Not necessary to fling me a bone of hope, Moe. There's nothing much else I can do but wait, is there? But a year? No—I doubt if I can be apart from you that long. . . . I may come crawling back to Europe far sooner, settle for being your excess baggage. See what I can settle for? How you effect me, Moe the fly-boy? I don't even have pride left. Still, when you boil pride down it's a petty, shallow thing. . . . I guess."

"Honey stop it, you're making me feel like a slob of a monster. You'll have me bawling, too, next." The really tremendous thing—which almost made me admire Valerie as much as I desired her—she DIDN'T turn on the tears. There and then, if she had cried, I think I would have bought that house in Kew Gardens.

Now, reaching my hotel room, I oiled and brushed my

119

hair, started to dress. I was damn glad I was still single. The big adventure I always knew waited for me some place—was about to start. What a dummy I'd have been to 'settle' for the steady job, driving a lawn mower instead of my own yacht.

I took a few shirts, packed a small bag. Glancing around my room I grinned at the Swiss coin I'd tossed hours earlier—to decide if I'd fly up to see Valerie—lying on the dresser top.

The old coin must be a counterfeit, it had given me a bum steer, a . . . I was about to pocket it but my hand stopped in mid-air. I remembered, it had landed heads, heads I'd see Valerie and it had come up heads.

But now it was tails up.

The maid had finished the room before I tossed . . . somebody had been in here, somebody had searched my room.

CHAPTER 3

I went over the room carefully and fast. There wasn't much to look for: sports jacket, a couple of shirts, slacks, flying jacket, odds and ends of shoes and shorts—all my worldly possessions. Everything was there, including the pocket of my raincoat turned inside out. It didn't make a bit of sense—what the devil did anybody hope—or expect—to find? Yet the room *had* been searched, the coin turned over. The door lock wasn't much, any punk lock-pick could open it in a second and . . .

A loud knock on the door made me jump. I flung it open to see Jimmy Johnson's long kisser grinning at me. Walking into the room he said, "They gave me your room number downstairs, Kelly. Man, you have a nice pad here, working for an oil company is okay. Ready to blow?" He was dressed in worn dungarees, dark polo shirt, heavy work shoes, with a battered brown camera case hanging from his thick neck.

"I'm ready." It was odd the desk clerk hadn't phoned the room before sending Johnson up. But Jimmy couldn't have searched my room, we'd been together in Pisa. "You get the crowbars?"

"No. Hard to find in Viareggio. I'll buy 'em in Milano. If you have stronger shoes than those loafers, wear 'em—we'll be working in rock. And take a sweater, mountains turn cold at night."

I changed into tough flying boots, threw my flying jacket into the little bag. As I opened the door he asked, "Where's your camera, Kelly?"

"Camera?"

"Come on, you don't look the tourist square without a camera. I picked up this Leica for a carton of cigarettes during the war."

"Let's not overdo the tourist act—I haven't a camera," I told him, opening the door.

Johnson picked up the coin on the dresser. "Leaving this for the maid? Swiss money is tops in value, but this ain't much of a tip."

"It's my good luck coin—I hope," I said, taking it from his heavy hand—wondering why I bothered to lock the door. Downstairs I handed the key to the desk clerk, told him I was off to Rome for a few days. When I tossed my bag into the back of the Fiat, Johnson said, "Not checking out was playing it smart—won't arouse any suspicion."

I nodded, saw Jimmy had ropes, short trench shovels, pick, a couple of packages, plus a new and cheap suitcase in the station wagon.

Mussolini—for military reasons—made Italy famous for its roads 25 years before we had throughways in the States. I knocked off an even 60 an hour on the *autostrada* all the way to Milan.

Like all compulsive talkers, Johnson lacked a sense of humor. After an hour's driving my knee began to ache and when I rubbed it, I had to explain about hurting the knee in a football game. Johnson took off on: "In the 1928 World Series the Babe didn't clout a homer in the first three

121

games, which the Yanks won. Ruth had a sore knee, like you. Even though he collected a couple of hits, the fans kept riding the Babe to smack a four-bagger. Man, in the fourth game old Babe hit three homers as the Yanks swept the series!"

"Makes my knee feel better already," I told him, watching his thick face in the windshield mirror. The sarcasm was lost on him.

It seemed Jimmy was also a horse player and when he started blabbing about this and that race, I cut him off with, "The only time I saw the bangtails run—I took a bath." In the windshield mirror his face turned so dumb and blank, I had to keep from laughing.

But talk helped pass the time and we did get into one mild argument, which puzzled me. Jimmy was gassing about his favorite subject, baseball, and my mind was full of Marisa, when he said, "They don't have any decent outfielders any more. When DiMaggio retired they threw away the mold."

He evidently expected some kind of an answer to this deep remark, so I said, "I don't know about that, when it comes to all-around fielding there's no flies on Willie Mays." I smiled at my own pun.

He screwed up his ugly face. "Aw, he's no good, he's colored."

I studied his face in the mirror to see if Johnson was kidding: he wasn't. For a time I did crop-dusting in the deep South and never heard even the most rabid member of the White Citizens Council doubt Willie Mays' ability as a baseball great.

I was about to tell him that was dumb thinking, but why argue with a joker cutting me in on a million? An Italian version of a Piper Cub passed about a thousand feet over us. The plane banked and flew over our station wagon again, coming down to maybe 200 feet. I asked Johnson, "That a police plane spotting us?"

"How could they possibly know? Did you tell anybody about this?"

"No."

He stuck his blonde-bald head out the window for a better look at the plane, now disappearing off to our right.

"Don't see any government markings on the wing. Just a private sports plane."

"The bastard almost buzzed us."

Johnson laughed. "The Italians are show-offs. They were lousy soldiers, but their air force was first rate and daring —because they loved to show off."

But from then on I had this feeling we were being watched. I kept telling myself it was dumb thinking, but the feeling remained with me. To change the subject I asked, "If we should find the chests, what do you think they'll contain?"

"Man, I told you—millions!"

"I mean, what will the loot be in—Italian paper money?"

"Probably some of that—it still spends."

"But if it's in large bills, won't we have a hard time changing them?"

"Don't worry, Kelly, a guy on the lam, like Il Duce was, must have thought of that, too. There probably will be gold bars, money in gold and paper, even some famous paintings, great jewels. Crazy isn't it, a ruby or a diamond, which has no practical use, always keeps its value, despite wars, revolutions, or what have you."

"But how do we dispose of jewels, especially famous ones?"

Jimmy asked sharply, "Growing cold on our deal, Kelly?"

For an answer I gunned the Fiat to top speed. "No, it's just that if we find jewels and gold bars, it may be messy converting them into cash, take a lot of time." I almost added, "And they say European jails are real bad."

"What if it does take time? Once we get the loot out of Italy, it's all ours—legally."

"You certain about that? Italy and France probably have extradition agreements, and Interpol is an international police force. I'd hate to be on the run from them."

"Even with millions?" Johnson asked, as if it was all a big joke.

"There's no point in being the richest chumps in jail."

"Kelly, don't let it bug you, all we have to worry about is first finding the loot, then flying it out of Italy. Legally it's finders-keepers, outside of Italy. Gold and jewels are constantly in demand, always a black market for them. I've made a few quiet inquiries, know where to dispose of the stuff—once we find it."

"You've spent a lot of time on this."

Johnson laughed. "Man, I haven't thought of anything else these last few years! Don't worry, I've covered all possible angles."

But it struck me as odd he hadn't figured the most important angle of all—how to get the loot out of Italy. That would be the *first* thing I would have worked out. Still, there was a reasonable answer to that. As a postal clerk, Johnson couldn't possibly save or raise enough money to buy his own plane, hire a pilot, or a fair-sized boat . . . the only two ways of taking the treasure out of Italy. Here I was stewing over how we'd sell the loot, and we might never even find it.

As we neared Milan the traffic grew heavier. A motorcycle passed us, the driver wearing wide goggles and a black crash helmet. He was bent over the handles, like a race driver, but I had a fast look at the side of his face and damn if I didn't see a half-moon scar on his right cheek! I pushed the gas pedal to the floor, trying to catch him, but he had too much speed for the light Fiat.

As I cut in and out of traffic, Johnson looked at me with alarm. "What the hell you doing, Kelly? They have motor cops on these roads, and let's not get into an accident *before* we have our chance to hunt for the cave!"

"Yeah," I grunted, letting our speed drift down to 60.

"If you're tired, I'll drive."

"I'm okay. That guy who passed on the motorcycle, I . . . thought I saw a scar on his face, like the scar-face who put my boss in the hospital."

"What? Great Gordon Gin, you turning jittery on me, Kelly?"

"Don't worry about me."

"Okay, okay, but be careful, I don't want the police getting curious about us, for any reason. And forget your boss—we're in business for ourselves, now!"

It was twilight when we entered Milan. Johnson had me park while he went to buy crowbars. "No sense anybody seeing two Yanks together, and remembering the license of the car. Tourists don't buy crowbars, but I can pass as Italian."

I nodded, got out to stretch my legs. There was a little bar across the street and I told Johnson I'd have a beer waiting for him.

"Don't get stoned."

"I never drink—except for an occasional brew."

Johnson slapped me on the back, a patronizing gesture which annoyed the hell out of me, for some reason. "Good boy. There's no such thing as the 'bottle of courage.' When I return we'll knock-off a big meal—lot of hard work ahead of us. Keep an eye on the car, these Eye-ties will steal even the time of day."

I had a cold beer, sitting by the window where I could see the station wagon. I was jumpy—Johnson was starting to get on my nerves with all his stupid chatter—plus I still had this strong feeling we were being followed. Be a great old deal if we acted as bird dogs for the Italian government, were tossed into the clink for our trouble. That would be adventure with a tiny 'a,' leaving me minus a job, money, Marisa . . . and Valerie.

Milan is a fine city, large and modern, and the few times I've been in Milan it has always reminded me of Long Island City. The bar began to fill with factory workers stopping for their *birra,* or an aperitif, before heading home for supper. I was the only 'foreigner' in the joint and it seemed to me that over the chatter of fast Italian, the music blaring from a radio perched at one end of the bar . . . they were all watching me.

I knew that was nutty, my imagination, but there was one guy in greasy cover-alls, tall and lean, who really kept looking my way, mumbling in his brandy, dark eyes mean and wild. He finally made some loud crack, something about mothers and Americans, and the other drinkers told him to shut up. All of which started a great deal of fast and furious Italian going.

I knew damn well, what little I could understand, he was talking about me. I told myself to cool it, wondered what was keeping Jimmy. Of course I could simply leave the bar, wait at the car. But I wasn't going to do that—I don't like being pushed around.

Now the tall guy broke away from his bar buddies, walked to my table, glowering and sputtering. Whatever he was drinking was sweet, there was stale-sweet odor to his words as he mentioned mothers again, Americans, and Foggia—a town in southern Italy with a fine air field. He also had his right hand on the back pocket of his work pants. The bartender came over to talk to the guy, who pointed an angry finger at me and yelled a curse of some kind. The bartender, an elderly man with a hell of a wave to his thick grey hair, turned to me and said in broken English, "This man . . . he upset . . . no like your fly shoes. He say *Americani . . . soldati* bomb house Foggia . . . in war. . . kill his mama. You . . . see?"

I nodded. "Tell him I wasn't out of my baby clothes when Foggia was bombed. Also tell him I'm pretty steamed myself—Christopher Columbus' men killed my great-great-great grand uncle, who was an Indian. So we're even."

I shouldn't have clowned, the bartender, lost in my English, mumbled, "Columbus of Genoa?" and looked troubled.

A little man with a grey goatee and fancy trimmed moustache, wearing old but clean overalls, left the bar . . . laughing . . . to translate what I'd said to the tall guy—who didn't think it funny, but got the picture. The bearded man turned to me. "Kindly pay no heed to this one, he is zig-zag drunk."

The neat way he spoke English reminded me of Marisa. "Tell him I'm sorry about his mother, but I didn't start the war."

"Yes, I shall so inform him. I myself, in the name of all Italy, apologize for what Columbus did to your Indian uncle." He slipped me a mock bow, then added, "Of what tribe was your uncle? I have seen many of your western motion pictures. They also killed many Indians."

"Yeah, it's rough being a movie Indian. My great uncle was of the Screwoff tribe." I wasn't entirely clowning, there is some Mohawk blood in our family tree.

"A most noble tribe of warriers," the goatte said. He started to walk the tall guy back to the bar, but the joker broke loose and in a hysterical voice snarled something at me, spit on my boots. I didn't mind the spit—the boots were dirty—but I knew enough Italian to understand he was talking about mothers again—*my* mother!

As I jumped to my feet, the tall guy's hand raced back to his hip pocket, but my left hook reached his jaw first—

126

he was wide open. He was stiff as he pitched forward, hit the hard floor.

The man with the goatee stared up at me with shocked eyes, said coldly, "He was only zig-zag, why you punch him? And so hard?"

"Balls, that wasn't any cocktail he was about to pull out of his back pocket!" I snapped. The silence in the bar was like a blanket, a dozen hostile eyes glaring at me. Maybe not exactly hostile—more like they were looking at garbage.

Bending down cautiously I turned the stiff over, felt of his back pocket—pulled out a small pen knife. It wasn't much, but still a knife. Pointing to it I told the goatee, "If you think I was going to stand still for that, you're all sick in the head!"

"He was zig-zag, an older man less in weight than you. He was only talk, meant no harm you." The goatee knelt beside the man, felt his pulse, stroked his face. "You hit most hard, but he come around. To knock man down before his friends, that is bad thing. But he was very zig-zag, and that very bad thing for you, *Signore* Indian. You act more like bad cowboy—you no Indian."

I glanced around the bar slowly, wishing one of the others staring at me would start something, as I rubbed the knuckles of my left hand—still sore from last night. I stood there for a long moment, then walked out. The guy I'd slugged was sitting up, shaking his head and moaning.

Johnson was standing beside our Fiat across the street, looking like an ugly Christmas tree in the dim light with a couple of short crowbars in his left hand, the camera hanging from his neck, small carton of groceries tucked under his right arm, and a paper bag at his big feet. "Unlock the damn door so I can put this stuff in!" he said fiercely. "We got to scram before the police come. You off your rocker, Kelly?"

As I opened the doors I said, "Some drunken slob called me a son of a bitch."

Johnson put his things in the back, jumped in fast as I stepped on the starter. "Drive! What's with you—blowing a million bucks because of a few goddamn words!"

I edged out into the traffic. "Which way?" I was so steamed I was ready to belt his long, tempting jaw if he said anything. But mostly I was angry at myself—all my life I'd looked forward to an adventure like this, and 1 was acting like a jittery amateur.

"Toward the center of town, want to find us a decent restaurant. Kelly, watch your lousy temper or. . . ."

"Or what?" I snarled.

Jimmy's tough face tightened, then he sighed, fingered the ring of yellow hair around his bald dome. "Kelly, for a million bucks I'd let anybody curse my family all night long."

"That's you, not me!"

"Relax. We're trying like hell not to attract attention and you fall into another brawl. Grow up, Kelly."

"I don't take any . . . !"

"All right, forget it—no damage done, but keep your mind on the job. I've brought chow—in case we don't want to, or can't, stop for grub in the morning. I think of everything."

"Yeah? You look like a damn tourist with that camera slung from your neck—a tourist buying crowbars!"

"There's a nice restaurant over there—park where we can keep an eye on the car. Calm down, Kelly, it's over. If you're going to be a millionaire, start thinking like one—a wealthy cat never fights himself, he hires somebody to do it for him. Let's eat—I'm starved."

The food was okay but I wasn't hungry. I had this feeling of being mixed-up in something . . . unknown; a chump walking into a strange swamp, aware there's quicksand about, but not where. Johnson ate like there was no tomorrow. Between stuffing his big mouth and talking about what Dusty Rhodes did in the '54 World Series, or the perfect game Don Larson hurled, he'd urge me to: "Come on, Kelly, shovel food in—you'll need all your energy tonight."

I picked at my food uneasily. Once, through the window, I was certain Marisa rode by on a scooter—a girl with long dark hair, white blouse, a flash of the same vivacious face. Not having time to run out, make sure, I wondered if my nerves were blowing.

I was glad when we were on rubber again, Johnson at the wheel, belching happily as we headed north. It was a perfect night, cool, full moon, the roads practically empty. We sped through several small villages, neat and silent as a postal card picture, with the moon spotlighting the mild pastel colors of the small houses. We rarely saw a lit window. "They sure pull in the sidewalks here at 9 P.M."

"Hope so," Johnson grunted. "We don't want company."

An hour later, passing the same rusty-pink house twice, I knew we were riding in circles, asked Johnson if he was lost. "Know what I'm doing. Making sure we're not being followed."

"You have this feeling about being tailed, too?"

He shook his head. "No. We haven't even passed another car in the last 20 minutes, but if the Italian government does know what we're up to, they'll have to make a move now, and on these empty roads we should be able to spot them. Watch it, now." He suddenly turned off the paved road, stopped the Fiat. For a dozen minutes we sat in silence, listening hard. All I heard were the usual insect noises of the country, a few mosquitos buzzing us.

There wasn't a house or shack of any kind in sight. On the other side of the road a mountain rose high above us. Our side was lined with a layer of thick woods. Northwest of us were the Alps, topped by silver-white clouds of fog and snow, the jagged peaks seeming to touch the moon.

Johnson motioned for me to follow him out of the car. I flexed my arms, as if I was entering the ring. He whispered, "In case people or a car should pass and stop, we've had motor trouble."

I nodded. "This the spot?"

"Near here," he said, taking a roll of black tape from his back pocket, covered both our headlights, leaving only a thin slit. Snapping on the lights he drove ahead for a few minutes, suddenly turned the little station wagon directly into the woods. We crawled and bumped along, the headlight slits giving only a faint light in the gloomy darkness. We weren't following a road, not even a path. I told him, "Careful, you'll rip out the transmission."

"With your cut of the loot you can buy out the auto rental agency."

"Wasn't thinking of that—we'll need the car to bring the stuff back to the Pisa airport."

Johnson nodded. "I forgot that. Take one of the crowbars and walk ahead, push any rocks and tree trunks aside. Watch out for snakes."

Walking in front of the Fiat on the fringe of the dim light from our slit headlights, sweating and stumbling as I pushed rocks aside—I had this weird feeling Johnson was about to run me over. It was a dumb hunch; he was crawling so slowly in an hour we had covered less than a hundred yards. Then the trees became so thick it was impossible to drive farther.

Johnson got out, whispered, "We walk from here. Isn't far. On the other side of these damn trees the ground slopes to the valley. The cave is on the slope."

We divided the ropes, shovels, crowbars, the other packages. I locked the Fiat, took the keys. He covered a flash with his thick hand, and we stumbled through the heavy woods. It was rugged going and my knee began to hurt. I couldn't see how we would ever carry the hundred treasure chests back to the station wagon, or how Musso's men had managed to lug them into these woods while on the run from. . . .

Like a curtain parting, we stepped out into bright moonlight on the side of a steep hill. There was a breath-taking scene about half a mile below—for an artist—a jigsaw of flat wheat fields, a breeze rippling through to make wavy lines. But there wasn't anything even looking like a farm house in sight. When we stopped to rest I pulled out a pack of cigarettes. Johnson snapped, "No lights! A match can be seen miles from here."

We moved to our right along the side of the hill, the slope so sharp a false step would send us tumbling. It was clumsy going carrying the tools, and again I wondered how in hell we'd make it back with heavy chests. We were both sweating like slobs and, after crawling along for some 20 minutes, Johnson stopped before a slight mound heavy with weeds and low bushes, said, "Well, here she is."

"*This?* You said they dynamited a cave to close it with rocks. Not a rock here."

"The years have covered it with dirt. Any blast makes good fertilizer—adds nitrogen to the soil. Notice how the bushes are thicker here. We'll take turns working."

He grabbed a shovel and began digging into the side of the hill, mountain, or whatever we were standing on. Working hard, Johnson cleared a spot some 10 feet wide of brush before he handed me the trench shovel.

The ground was tough. Although the night was cool, I was soon bathed in sweat, took off my shirt. The deeper I dug the harder the earth. About the time I was convinced we were busting our backs for nothing, my shovel hit rock —jagged rocks, such as an explosion might make.

Johnson took over as I rested, working the rocks loose with a crowbar, handing them out. He told me, "Don't let them roll down the hill, make a racket." Although his shirt was so wet I could see the movement of his back muscles, he still had his silly camera dangling from around his bull neck.

At 1 A.M. we stopped to eat, our clothes torn and dirty, the night really cold. We had a hole 6 feet deep, funneling to a point where the digger had to squat and my bum knee was killing me. I asked, "How the hell deep do we have to go?"

He shrugged.

"Certain this is the spot? I'm hardly up to tunneling across Italy, into Venice. What happens when it turns light?"

"We sleep, pray nobody notices our hole. I've brought netting to camouflage the opening. Anyway, too early in the season for farmers to be harvesting the fields down there. Let's have a go at it again."

Crawling into the hole I began making like a mole, my mind a tired fog. Working my fingers into the dark earth I wondered what I'd do if I came upon a snake? I remembered movies of guys tunneling their way out of a jail— we were working our way *in*, could be buried alive.

My knee wouldn't let me work in the cramped position for more than 5 minutes. When I crawled out, stretched on the cool ground, Johnson went into the hole. Moments later I heard his triumphant grunt: "Kelly!"

Squeezing in beside his sweaty body I saw the break-through, the cave opening . . . a ragged hole the size of my fist! Flashing his light into the stale darkness we saw several small trunks. I was so excited I forgot my knee— we began digging with our hands like frightened rats. The work was easier, pushing the dirt and rocks ahead of us, into the cave. We soon had a hole large enough for a man to push through and I followed Johnson into the cave—it was a small affair, maybe 15 feet deep with not enough headroom to stand.

Neither of us said a word as Johnson ran his flash over the trunks—they looked old and battered, made of a dull metal with two heavy metal bands and locks running around each trunk. There were only three chests. I asked, "Thought you read there were a hundred of 'em?"

"That's what the article stated." He sent the light bouncing about the cave. I suddenly saw the flash of two shining eyes—those of some large animal, a snake—in the darkness at one side of the cave! Grabbing Johnson's hand I turned the flash back in that direction. . . . We saw two skeletons in the rotted, powdered, remains of olive-green Italian army uniforms, the gaping eye sockets of the skulls giving me a bad turn. Ankle bones disappeared into a mess which had been shoes, while one skull still held a kind of cap at a rakish angle. What I'd taken for 'eyes' were the metal handles of knives, one in each rotting belt around the hip bones, the blades covered by crumpling leather sheaths.

Walking toward the bones Johnson said, "As in the days of pirates, these poor bastards probably lugged the trunks in and were killed in the blast—to make sure the location remained a secret. See the crazy angles of their arms and legs? Man, these cats were blown against the side of the cave!"

I touched one of the knife handles—the fascist fasces emblem like something kids get with a box-top. Except for a fine layer of dust, the knife was cool and clean to my touch.

"Come on, nothing they can do to us. Let's try lifting the trunks," Johnson said, turning his flash back to the caskets.

The leather handles powdered in our hands but by scooping dirt out from under each end, we managed to raise one trunk a few inches off the ground. I figured it weighed at least 300 pounds.

We put it down, wiped the sweat from our faces as Johnson chuckled, said happily, "Gold is so damn heavy!"

Taking the flash, I knelt and peered into a tiny hole— where part of a leather handle had been attached—saw something which glittered in my light. I held the flash while

Johnson took a peek. He grinned. "Jewels! What's the matter, Kelly, you think they'd bury pop-corn?"

"Only wanted to make sure."

"You can be sure we've a fortune! We'll enlarge the cave opening, then put a rope around each trunk, pull it out."

We widened the hole in no time, roped the first trunk— then crawling out into the welcome cold of the night we strained and sweated—and couldn't move it! My knee was folding and I finally had to tell Johnson I'd had it. Yanking his wrist watch from a pants pocket, he said, "We haven't much time, be light in a couple hours."

"We'll never lug the trunks out. Let's open them, take what we can in our hands, cover the opening of the cave. We'll return later for the rest."

Johnson shook his head, gave me an ugly smile. "Return when? Gold is even heavier with greed—we'd spend all our time watching the other for a double-cross."

"Even if we manage to get them out of the cave, how are we going to carry the trunks along this steep hillside, through all those damn woods, to the car? We need a derrick to lift them. . . ."

Jimmy held up a thick hand. "Man, you just hit it! We've been working this like squares. Come on, Kelly!"

I followed him up the hill, into the woods. He grabbed a branch about 4 inches thick and a couple feet long. We both swung on it until the branch snapped. Johnson said, "Go get the knife from the dead men—they won't mind. I'll get a knife myself, take too long with your bum knee. Did I tell you the time Babe Ruth had. . . . ?"

"You told me. What's the knife for?"

"Show you in a second," Johnson said rushing through the woods and down the hill, as if about to kill himself. I leaned against the tree, feeling great. We weren't home yet, but we had it made—adventure had finally paid off—as I always knew it would. One night's hard work and ease for the rest of my. . . .

Jimmy came puffing up the hill, the knife blade flashing in the moonlight. "We're running in luck, Kelly. This is good steel, still razor-sharp." He cut the branch from the tree, then pointed the thicker end. Jimmy stuck the knife in his belt and we went back down to the cave. Outside the entrance he told me to dig a hole with a crowbar and stuck

133

the branch in, then pounded it with a shovel until about a foot of the wood was buried. Taking the end of the rope, which was still tied about one of the trunks, he ran the rope around the branch sticking out of the ground. Very much the in-charge-guy, Johnson told me, "We now have a kind of block and tackle deal, be easier to pull the chest out. Take the flash and you'll find a jar of honey in the food box—smear it on the post, act as a kind of grease."

I poured half of the jar on the post, making a sticky mess. We grabbed the rope and began pulling it around the pole. It was still tough but far easier than before. With much sweating and grunting, my knee hurting as if it was coming off, we finally pulled the first trunk out of the cave.

I was surprised it hadn't come apart with all that tugging. Panting and grinning, Johnson sat on the chest, told me, "See how simple life is when you use your brains, Kelly?"

"Okay, you're a whiz-kid. But I still don't see how we'll ever lug these back to the station wagon. We'll have to open them and make a number of trips with. . . ."

Johnson suddenly hit my arm, hissed, "Shhh! I hear . . . something!"

"Hear what?"

"Shut up—somebody's coming! Damn our luck!" He yanked the Italian knife from his belt, shoved the flashlight into my hand.

For a deep second we both listened hard, not breathing. Then I heard it too—steps in the woods coming our way, sound of branches being pushed aside. Johnson pulled my head toward his big mouth, whispered, "Kelly—get over on the other side of the cave opening, I'll be up higher— above the cave. Whoever's coming will have to make it slowly crossing the side of the hill. When you hear me whistle, turn on the flash—I'll jump 'em!"

"Okay. I'll flash the light and we'll both come rushing, send them tumbling down the hill!" I crawled over beyond the cave entrance, pointed the flash toward the faint trail we'd made at right angles to the slope; heard Johnson swiftly climbing up above me. Poking in the dirt we'd shoveled out, I picked a couple rocks of baseball size, put them at my side.

In the early morning the moon wasn't as high nor bright as before but soon I saw the dark figure of a man making his

134

way carefully across the steep side of the hill, towards us. He seemed to be short and stocky, stooped, walking boldly and loudly. I realized he probably didn't know we were there, might go by without even seeing us or our digging. But there was the rope coming out of the cave to the post—he'd certainly trip over that. Besides, why the devil would anybody be walking along this lonely hill in the dark of night, unless he knew of the cave? Or was he a cop? But our luck wasn't all bad—he was alone, we could tie him up, keep him on ice until we had the loot in the car, were on our way.

When the man was almost on the cave I heard Johnson's faint whistle, pressed the flash button. I saw a plump man wearing a black leather cycle helmet, a thick dark sweater, riding breeches and high black boots making his bowed legs look comical. He stopped, straightened up as he blinked at my light. He opened his little mouth and there was this *swish* sound in the stillness as Johnson's knife came flashing across the light, buried itself to the hilt in the dark sweater above the man's heart! He started to clutch at his belly, both hands crawling up the sweater toward the knife, then he bent over, fell on his face.

I heard a strange voice, shrill with fright, screaming, "What did you kill him for?" as I ran forward, my light still on. It took me a split second to realize it was my own voice.

Johnson came crashing down the hill, crying hoarsely, "Turn off that damn light!"

I cupped the flash with my hand and when I reached the man I opened my fingers to let a slit of light show the tiny stream of very red blood already snaking out from under the body.

Johnson stopped himself by sitting, sliding to a halt on his big behind. As he got to his feet, I heard myself say, "He doesn't look like an Italian cop," and with my left hand turned the dead man over.

I saw a lot of little things all at the same time:

—There was blood on the fasces emblem at the knife hilt.
—Wisps of dirty grey hair stuck out of the helmet.
—The slit mouth was wide open, like a fish trying to shake the hook.

—Blood and dirt were on the thin lips, the bad teeth.
—The nose was sharp and the hard eyes ready to pop
from the dead face.
—And on the waxen right cheek an old scar in the shape
of a ragged half-moon.

CHAPTER 4

"What the hell you think you're pulling on me, Kelly?"
Johnson's harsh voice hit me like a wallop, I don't like
anybody standing over me, especially Johnson. I stood up
fast, let the flash go off. I tried to make my voice sound
hard as I asked, "What's that slop supposed to mean,
Johnson?"

We were facing each other, over the dead man. "That
you must have shot-off your stupid mouth about us!" Johnson said, his odd twang heavy. "You tell me a guy with a
scar on his face was in an accident with your boss and the
next thing I know, the scar-face appears on this hillside!
Hell of a coincidence, isn't it, Kelly?"

"It sure is, but I don't know who this guy is—was. If
you hadn't lost your nerve, hadn't been so quick with that
cheese sticker, we might have found out what's back of
this."

"You saying you don't know him, never told him about
the treasure?"

"That's right," I said, my eyes on his hands.

"Maybe you and this creep were in on a deal to kill your
boss?"

"You're out of your humpty-dumpty mind!" I said,
coldly.

Johnson shrugged thick shoulders. "Hard to believe, but
I have to buy it. Besides, when we practically have the loot

in our hands, there's no sense arguing over a stranger, and a dead one at that. We'll forget it." Johnson said all this as if he'd merely flattened the man.

A fast wave of nausea raced through me and I had to fight against being sick. It wasn't the sight of the dead man at my feet, I once saw a mechanic sucked into a jet engine and he was a far worse mess than this. But a man had been killed in cold blood and sure as God made green apples, I was an accessory to murder!

Johnson reached over to shake me, I ducked back, growled, "Watch your hands!"

He said, "Easy, Kelly. Let's get him inside the cave, see who he is." Johnson took his shoulders, I picked up his legs, the leather of the boots soft and well cared for. We put him beside the two skeletons and I held the flash while Johnson went through his pockets, peeled the helmet from the dead man's head. There was a lot of wild, bushy, grey hair and scar-face suddenly became a fat old man, silly in his wide breeches, the thin knees, over-large boots. The open mouth added to the evil of his face, but the marble-hard eyes still seemed to be glaring at me. I turned away, looked down at the gaping skulls of the Italian soldiers. Something very vague about them tried to pierce the dull fog my brain was floating in. Something wrong. . . .

Johnson, squatting beside the old man, held up an identity card. "Says he's Andre Gabon, of Nice. Been to Nice, Kelly?"

"Yes."

"So . . . !"

"And to almost every other large European city, too."

"Nothing else much on him. Few keys, 10,000 lira, this hunk of paper which looks like a laundry ticket. And this." Johnson bounced a small automatic about on his large hand. He stuffed the money and paper into his pocket, dropped the gun on a rock, picked up another rock and smashed the little automatic. Then he grinned up at me, his damn camera case swinging from his neck like a pendulum above the knife in the dead man, said, "Best that way, big money does small things to men. Like us accusing each other of the double X merely because a stranger walked in on us. Well, he seems to be a loner, but let's get on with our work, faster, in case he had friends. Be light soon."

137

As Johnson stood up I asked, "What—what are we going to do with . . . him?"

"Leave him in the cave, a do-it-yourself tomb. Untie the rope on the trunk outside, we haul another one out."

I was glad to get moving. Perhaps because we knew how to do it now, the second chest came out with less tugging. I was still in a mental haze. Two thoughts kept pounding about in my numb head. There was the big thought: I'D KILLED A MAN! And a small but sharper thought: there was something phony about all this, something I didn't understand. This second thought was riding topheavy on a tiny item tickling the back of my mind—the cave had changed, somehow. I didn't know *what* had changed—but something was very wrong.

As we were resting on the second trunk, the cold night air a bracer, I asked, "Why did you knife him? He was alone, we could have jumped him easily, learned what he was doing here."

"Safely? You saw the rod, he might have shot or wounded one of us. In the good crime movies, it's always a little thing like a gun falling, the bullet bouncing off a wall, which trips up the. . . ."

"Nuts, this isn't a movie! We could have handled a little fat old man!"

"Kelly, we're on top of a treasure which hasn't been touched in nearly 20 years—suddenly a guy walks in on us. What else could we have done with him, but knock him off, sooner or later?"

"You don't kill just because you have your mitts on millions," I mumbled, confused.

Johnson chuckled. "Come on, Kelly, men are dying every second, don't go soft on me. Damn right you don't kill for millions—usually a man kills for peanuts in some punk stick-up, or over a dumb argument! During the war, I killed for glory, for two-bit medals. What's eating you, want out?"

"No. But I didn't plan on murder."

"Exactly what were your plans? To ease me out? You're the one hooked up with this guy. . . . See, there we go again, fighting between ourselves. Forget him, he was old, might have had a heart attack if we jumped him. When we fill up

138

the cave entrance, he'll never be found. Let's get cracking on the last trunk."

The third chest seemed heavier than the other two. Opening a can of thick, syrupy peaches, we used the juice as 'grease' for the rope. Dawn was streaking the sky a dull grey when we finally pulled the last trunk outside.

Sitting next to our loot, we ate sandwiches, drank bottles of warm mineral water. The valley below was quiet and peaceful, the rising sun flicking the fields with gold.

After we filled the cave as best we could with loose dirt and rocks, humming softly to himself, Johnson took out some folded netting, flung it over the cave entrance. We tossed bushes on top of the netting and I had to admit it was a good job of disguise. I told him, "Be difficult to spot this from below, or from the air."

"You learn many things in war, like. . . . *Air!* Kelly, you hit on our answer!"

I gave him a blank look.

"Man, see the field directly below us—the wheat is only a foot high, the field smooth!"

"So what?"

"Kelly, wake up, you're a pilot! The field is about 1200 feet long, plenty of space for you to put your Cessna Twin down and take off! As you said, it will be rugged and maybe take days for us to lug the trunks back to the Fiat. But with more rope, cans of grease, it'll be a snap to lower the trunks to the field below! Listen, you drive the car back to Pisa— should make it before noon. Get some sleep and at 6 P.M. land your Cessna in the wheat field. Take us the rest of the night to get the trunks down, aboard the plane, but by 8 or 9 A.M. we're in France, wealthy men!"

I came awake so fast my head seemed to orbit! How dumb can one guy get? Taking it from the top, *I'd been had all the way!*

I was sure I could handle Johnson. We were the same weight but his muscles were made for lifting, not punching, plus I was half his age. Also, I can take a guy out with my right. But belting Johnson now meant giving up the loot— I sure couldn't get the chests out alone. I could flatten him, tie his hands and turn him over to the Italian cops . . . but I'd end in the can myself, or maybe dead, if they had the death penalty for killing over here. The very least I could expect, if I managed to skip jail, would be messy headlines, end of my soft job, any chance of the airline berth. Nor was I ready to give up the loot. An opportunity like this would never come again to. . . .

"What's wrong, Kelly, don't you buy my idea?"

I had to check on him again—maybe my weary noggin had heard wrong before. I said, "I'm thinking about it. At this high altitude—and with a heavy load—I'd need at least 1500 feet for take-off."

I wasn't wrong. Johnson said, "What heavy load? You have a five seater, meaning at least a 1000 pound pay-load. Including our own weight, we'll be under that. Forget the high altitude, it will be night time and cold, you won't need so long a run. Anyway, I said the field was 1200 feet— might be 1500—maybe even 2000. And it's been ploughed, when they planted the wheat, so all large rocks are gone. Even if you should crack-up the landing gear, we can still carry the loot to the road, buy a car. Or are you afraid of leaving me here with the chests?"

"Maybe I am."

Johnson threw his bald head back and chuckled—the laugh annoying me so much I had to rub my hands together to keep from slugging him. I knew damn well he was laughing at me. He said, "See what money does, Kelly? Up to the second we found the stuff we trusted each other, without question! Now—frankly I'm worried about you, you can blow the whistle on me, try for a reward from Rome."

"Will part of the reward be the firing squad, the hot seat, when they see the old man's corpse in the cave!"

The smug chuckle again—Johnson was having a high old time, a great inside joke. "Yes, you would have some explaining to do. All of which means we can trust each other because we have to! Great Gordon Gin, I can't move the trunks alone, and if I had anybody else in on the deal, any other way of taking the stuff out of Italy, I wouldn't have cut you in. So we trust the other because we have no other choice. Right?"

I nodded, almost smiling. He was a cute bastard, laying on the homey touch with 'Great Gordon Gin.' It was surprising he didn't continue with his baseball buff act, recite more of the record book. He was damn right about one fact—he was a thorough type—a thorough louse!

140

He asked, "You agree with my plan, Kelly?"

I nodded.

"Good. Are you sure you can find this field from the air? Remember, you'll have to fly in at dusk, so as not to attract attention. Let me draw a map for you on the side of this cracker box."

Johnson was an all-around; shielding the flash with his left hand, he drew a hell of a fine detailed map of the area. I wondered how often he had practiced drawing it. He told me, "When you circle the field, I'll flash this light four times and the moment you land, turn off your lights, wait at the plane for me. Okay?"

I pocketed the map. Still acting the innocent, I asked, "What if you have company during the day, Jimmy?"

He shrugged. "As the man says, you don't gamble you can't win. Unless your old buddy in there—I mean the stranger—was part of a gang, which I doubt or he wouldn't have come alone, there's little chance of anybody passing this way. Perhaps a farmer or a hunter—I'll handle that. That's what I mean—if you don't see the four flashes of my light, fly on. I'll contact you in Viareggio."

I didn't know whether to laugh, or spit in his sly puss—he'd be waiting for me, *waiting to kill me!*

Johnson stretched. "Sun will be out hot soon. We've put in a good night's work."

"Yeah, it's been quite a night."

"I'm going to get some shut-eye. You do the same when you reach Pisa."

I nodded, knew I had to get out of there at once—one more bit of patronizing advice and I'd slug the bastard. "Help me get the Fiat back on the road."

"Of course, Kelly. For the love of mike, don't talk to anybody. *Anybody!*"

I smiled in the early morning cold light at that 'love of mike,' even felt myself unwinding—a bit. I could picture Johnson rehearsing his role, the correct 'American expressions,' getting everything down to a 'T.' Being so damn cocky he didn't realize the dumb mistake he'd made. As the bastard had said, always some simple thing trips the most careful plans.

Walking through the woods we reached the Fiat, found scar-face's motorcycle alongside it: he'd been the same one

141

who had passed us on the road. We buried it under brush and leaves, then I backed the station wagon out, with Johnson walking ahead, guiding me. I had to fight the desire to run him over—call it an accident. Kent Kelly, boy adventurer! I'd sure walked into something right up to my dumb ears!

When we reached the road Johnson went over the map again, reminded me to buy plenty rope and grease—even gave me a story to tell any curious storekeeper—I needed rope because my yacht was stuck on a sandbar off some beach.

I started the car, watched Johnson disappear into the woods, via the rear view mirror. I felt a sharp relief at leaving him, then so depressed I thought I'd be sick. Now there was no evading a decision: to return or to pack the deal in. If I returned I had to figure out a way of taking Jimmy Johnson—even the name was carefully thought out —before he took me. I could return to Pisa, straighten up about the station wagon, fly up to Paris and see Valerie, pick up Mr. Moore next Tuesday—forget the entire business; leave Johnson sitting on the hillside with his loot.

But it wasn't that simple—if I didn't show tonight he'd come looking for me, watch Moore, perhaps try to get me through Moores' Italian in-laws. Even if he didn't go after them, it would still mean I was passing up millions. . . . I kept telling myself it wasn't a question of being money-crazy nor greedy, but being practical. I should have insisted we open one of the trunks, actually see the loot. While I was gone the clever bastard might fill them with rocks, bury the loot elsewhere? No, that would truly be a rock move— he'd been waiting patiently all these years for a chance to take the loot, and then I'd come along, Kelly the All-American dumb-ox with muscles for brains!

Passing a small lake I parked the Fiat and took a bare-ass swim to wash up, the chilly, early morning water a good shock. I brushed my clothes as best I could and in Milan stopped to buy a sport shirt and a cup of coffee.

Tooling along the *autostrada* toward Pisa I felt better, able to think clearly. One thing was for sure: I *was* involved in this mess, so there wasn't any point in running, or passing up the loot. If I ran, baldy might blame me for knifing the old man—the desk clerk at the Marchony, the auto rental people in Pisa—they had all seen us together.

Not running then presented a couple of problems: how to keep myself alive, what the hell to do with Johnson, and the loot. The last wasn't much of an immediate problem—it might take time to learn how to dispose of gold bars, jewels, painting, or whatever form the booty came in—but I'd have plenty of time once I flew it out of Italy. I could even rebury it again in France or England, take it slow.

What to do with Johnson was a real sharp burr under my pants and linked with keeping myself among the living. I knew now what had hit me wrong back in the cave—*both* knives from the skeletons were missing, meaning Johnson was keeping one to stick in my back. He was good at it—that had been a hell of an expert throw with the knife going right on target—scar-face's ticker. So I knew how I'd get it, but at least I had a small edge going for me—Johnson didn't know I was wise to him, everything had seemingly gone the way he wanted. The bastard even had me block up the cave again—before I might have taken off the old man's sweater, looked for tattoo markings in his armpit. But I hadn't known the score, then.

Johnson wouldn't go for me until we loaded the trunks on the Cessna, which would be a two-man job. What he had in his twisted mind was to wait until we were airborne—it would be a tricky take-off—then kill me and take my plane. I'd give odds he wouldn't fly to Paris, either!

All of which boiled things down for me: I had to take care of baldy *immediately after* we loaded the plane. That fixed the time, but 'take care' how? There was a very simple way—kill the bastard! Be easy enough to dump his body out over the Alps. Only person who would miss Johnson was scar-face. The gang that went through the act of jumping me in Viareggio, they could only have a hazy—if any—idea of what Johnson had in mind for me. Killing was the cleanest, the *only* way out for me.

The trouble with that was—I didn't think I could do it. I wanted adventure, action, excitement, but neither plain murder, or to be the partner of a super-killer!

If I didn't kill Johnson, then what? I could throw a gun on him, force him to open the chest, then I'd fly off with my share. But aside from the fact I didn't want the slob to get a penny of the blood-money, and that's what it would be

143

for *him,* if I left Johnson alive he'd spend the rest of his life, and his share of the loot, tracking me down. I couldn't enjoy the money if I had to keep looking over my shoulder every second.

I could tie him up, turn him over to the authorities in France. But again, that meant world headlines, and I might end up a hero—or on the wrong end of the stick. Despite the song and dance he'd slipped me about our legal right to the loot once it was out of Italy, I wasn't sure I could keep it. Headlines would mean big tax bites, complications—there were still too damn many Johnsons in high places the world over. I had to take the millions quietly, or not at all.

My mind kept kicking it around until my head was splitting and then I started to sweat, for no matter how I added, it always came out to one answer—kill him!

By the time I reached Pisa, returned the Fiat, I was sick from thinking *how* I'd murder him. More than anything else at the moment, I longed to talk it through with somebody—anybody. Valerie would merely scream at the idea, turn hysterical. But Marisa, she would understand my dilemma . . . and for a wild second I considered taking the bus to Viareggio. But I realized that was dumb thinking; murder calls for a lone hand.

Taking a taxi to the Pisa airport, I had the Cessna Twin rolled out of the hanger, the sweet, jet-swept lines with the wing-tip tanks giving me the usual charge. Stepping up on the wingwalk, I sat in the cabin, went through a routine check. There was a 12 inch prop clearance, so aside from chopping off some wheat tips, I'd be okay. I debated filling the reserve fuel tanks—every ounce of weight I could shed would make the take-off easier.

Staring at the instrument panel, sitting in my usual seat, calmed my nerves. Fuel and take-off weren't any real problems—nothing about flying worried me. What I had to do was cut the sloppy thinking, work out a plan. *Exactly how would I kill Johnson?* I probably could purchase a gun in Pisa, although I didn't even know if you needed a permit. A gun? Where would I pack it? Be simple enough to keep it in my flight jacket, but loading the trunks would be sweaty work, look suspicious if I kept my jacket on. I could hide it someplace in the cockpit, but Johnson would certainly case the plane for a gun. Wearing only slacks and a shirt, the bulge of a rod would be a snap to spot. Once he suspected I was wise to him, then that would throw the edge his way: he'd knock me off at once. Hell, he could always open the chests, load the plane by the handful—if he had to! But knowing Johnson's methodical mind, he'd rather do a neat job, load the trunks aboard—if he didn't think I was on to him.

Wouldn't be hard to carry an automatic inside my flight boots, but that meant a small caliber job, perhaps several shots, and Johnson was too fast with a knife for any miss on my part. True, I could pack a blade myself, it would lie flat in my pocket, but I'd never used one for anything more than peeling an orange, and this wasn't the time for amateur night.

My head was coming apart. Taking my tool box I walked out on the wing, jumped to the ground. Removing the cowling of one of the 260 h.p. engines, I picked up a wrench to check the. . . . There was my simple answer! Be natural to have a wrench in the cockpit. The moment the last trunk was aboard I'd split his bald head with this wrench.

That was it! Staring at the wrench in my hand I nearly threw up. But there wasn't any other way—bust his skull, dump the corpse over the Alps.

I guess I'd known *that* was the only answer from the moment Johnson made his slip.

I finished checking the engines, working like a robot, refusing to even think about the job ahead. I bought grease at the airport, explained about needing a lot of rope to secure some oil barrels I expected to take on soon. With the coils of rope and grease in the cockpit, the plane fueled, I was ready to take off . . . for murder. I could even grin at the melodramatic sound of the words as I said them half aloud.

My nerves were steady but it was only 3:15 P.M.—I had a couple of hours to waste. I went to the bar and ordered a whiskey neat, and couldn't finish it. Booze never did a thing for me. I had a sandwich and a couple cups of java, my nerves on fire. The hours seemed a lifetime. . . . I couldn't even kill time when it meant I was about to kill a man.

I went back to the plane, stretched out on the back seat.

145

Be simple enough to remove the seats. . . . I had been up over 48 hours, was bushed and exhausted, but I couldn't sleep.

I lay there, stewing, trying to convince myself I wanted the loot enough to murder. All the time I was sick with the thought that whether I wanted the loot or not, murder was still the only answer. . . . I'd boxed myself into a hell of a spot.

CHAPTER 5

Coming in at 350 feet to circle the wheat field, I saw the four quick flashes of Johnson's light on the side of the hill. Switching on my flush-mounted landing lights I started down, thinking how ironical it would be for both of us if I cracked up the Cessna—Johnson's careful plans shot to hell, while it would put an end to my worries about murdering him—if the crash didn't kill me.

I put her down gently, didn't roll as far as I expected, the wheat acting like a brake as the props chopped their way through the field. Turning off my lights I made certain *the* wrench was on the cockpit floor, under my seat within easy reach—even from the doorway. Then, taking off my flying jacket I opened my shirt, made sure nothing bulky was in my pants pockets, and waited.

Twilight was fast turning into night but I could still see well enough to watch Johnson come down the side of the steep hill with amazing speed—until I realized he was letting himself down with the rope. The last few hundred feet he moved slower—on his own.

I had the grease and ropes out, was waiting beside the plane when he came up. He had his flash tied to the straps of the sweaty camera case around his neck, and in the dim light I ran my eyes over his pants and shirt, looking for the knife. I didn't see its outline; he must have it in his socks. I knew he was frisking me with his eyes, too.

"Everything swinging okay, man?"

Tense as I was, I had a hard time not grinning at this corn. "Yeah. Things smooth here?"

He nodded. "Not a soul around. I've been pounding my ear most of the day. I feel great."

"Good for you. Let's walk to the end of the field, see how the ground is. When we're loaded any rock can blow a tire."

"Good idea. Just in case the sound of the plane circling brings anybody—we ran out of gas, had to make a forced landing."

We walked to the end of the wheat field and back, flushing a rabbit and a few small birds, maybe quail. The ground was smooth enough. Returning to the plane, Johnson followed me up the step to the wingwalk, inside the cabin, where we easily removed the seats from their track-mounts, stowed them in the rear of the cabin. The first stars were bright in the clear sky as we left the plane. Johnson lit a match to glance at his watch. Tossing the match away he said, "It's been an hour since you landed, the noise didn't bring anybody."

"The field is dry, watch the matches—whole deal will go up in smoke, including my plane."

Johnson nodded. "You're right, Kelly. That would be the wild card in the deck. Let's get cracking."

I kept watching his long, heavy jaw working as he talked. It seemed to fascinate me. Or perhaps I couldn't look at the skin stretched so tight over his big bald dome—knowing I'd soon have to split it.

He carried the cans of grease while I took the coils of rope, and my knee began aching after the first few feet of climbing up toward the cave. But once we reached the rope hanging from the wooden peg above, it was easy pulling myself up the hill.

With his usual efficiency, Johnson spliced the ends of the ropes I'd brought, then tested them and greased the wooden stump. We tied the first casket, lowered it down the hillside with little effort. My brain was awhirl with the pounding, nightmare thought I'd soon have to kill, and to get my mind off *that,* I thought of such fantastic things as—

147

what if one of the trunks got loose, busted open while we were lowering it—the harvest of gold and gems some astonished bastard would find on this slope . . . some day.

With the trunk at the bottom of the hill, we went down—guided by the rope—untied and carried the trunk the two or three hundred yards to the plane. This was back-breaking work with forced stops every few feet to rest the damn heavy casket. My knee was giving me hell and I was so bushed I moved in a mental fog, even grateful for each delay . . . it put off the act of murder. Johnson mumbled, "You should have landed the plane closer. Perhaps we can roll it . . ." He suddenly held up his right hand in the darkness.

Looking up from the casket I was sitting on, I rubbed the stubble on my chin, whispered, "What's up?"

Johnson pointed his hand at me, then held it up again—as if testing the wind. I couldn't hear a thing except the usual many country and night little noises. But I was too tired to hear well. I told myself to snap out of it, or I'd never be hearing anything again.

For a few minutes we were still, then he shrugged. "Thought I heard somebody moving out there, the swish of wheat. Let's go."

We lugged the chest another 50 feet when I had to call a halt again, my knee ready to break off while my back muscles seemed made of taffy. Johnson told me, smugly, I thought, "Take your time, Kelly, we have all night."

"Take us a year at this rate."

He chuckled. "Ain't bad pay for a year, is it, Kelly?" His voice sounded so much like that of a mid-Western yokel, for a confused moment I wondered if I could be all wrong. Was I about to kill an innocent chump?

When we finally reached my plane, lifting the trunk was pure torture. I was just too pooped to lift a damn thing. When I gave up on the second try, Johnson told me, "We'll leave it here, pile the chests on top of one another—make less lifting."

We walked back up the hills, which now seemed a vertical cliff to my aching knee. Reaching the spot in front of the cave where the two other chests stood, Johnson said, "Let me try lowering one alone while you rest."

"No, you'd never make it." I had visions—silly ones—

148

of him making a Herculean effort, getting the trunks aboard and flying off, leaving me sitting on the hillside like an idiot. "Give me a couple of minutes, I'll be okay."

"Of course, man."

Lowering the second trunk was a personal horror of pain —the rope burned my hands and I was panting so hard I thought my heart would pound to pieces against my rib cage. Then, oddly enough, while we were carrying the trunk across the field, I got my second wind, lost the punchy feeling. Now I was merely full of a dull dread, hearing over and over again in my mind—and so damn clearly—the sickening sound the wrench must make as it creased Johnson's skull—the sound branding me a murderer for the rest of my life.

Before lowering the last treasure chest, Johnson methodically cleaned up around the filled-in cave, scattering the empty food cans in the bushes.

I smoked a cigarette, shielding it with my open shirt, as he calmly made like a Boy Scout. I wondered how he could move so normally, knowing he planned to kill me within the next hour. I found myself almost admiring him, wishing I had his iron nerves.

Once the trunk was in the field Johnson expertly snapped the long rope as though it was a whip, neatly pulling it off the wooden peg high on the hillside. Coiling the rope, he tossed it on top of the trunk. Again, I could picture him practicing the stunt on some other hillside: he had every little move down to perfection.

The last chest seemed the heaviest and we were both puffing and sweating when we finally heaved it atop the other two. The night was hazy, a faint rain ring around the moon. Stepping up on the wingwalk, I snapped on the cabin light, pulled the window curtains shut. Johnson said to cut the light but I shook my head. "We have to chance it—a wrong shove with these heavy trunks might wreck the plane."

"Okay, you're the pilot, Kelly. If anybody was around, we'd have seen them by now."

We lifted and pushed the trunk aboard, made it as secure as we could. I kept seeing the wrench under the pilot's seat, my tense mind now a series of corny, flash headlines:

149

THE WRENCH WAS FOUND EMBEDDED IN THE DEAD MAN'S BRAINS!
KENT KELLY WANTED FOR MURDER!
"KILLED FOR MONEY," PILOT ADMITS.
AMERICAN PILOT EXECUTED IN ITALY FOR MURDER!

We rested but I couldn't stop sweating, nor staring at the wrench—its cold steel beauty soon to be covered with blood. Would a single blow do it, or would I have to hear the crunch of steel against bone again and again?

Johnson was sitting on the second trunk, the faint cabin light showing a smile on his ugly face. I was certain he knew what was going on in my mind, my fears. Was his grin a mocking leer . . . mocking my fear of killing?

We loaded the second trunk and I was very tired, my nerves ready to snap. Johnson was standing outside the plane, still smiling. Smacking a mosquito I snapped, "What the hell's so funny? What are you grinning about?"

"Relax, Kelly. Man, why shouldn't I smile? It's almost midnight—by morning we'll be rich."

"Where do we land in France?" I asked, stalling.

"Where do you usually put down? At Orly?"

Nodding . . . I suddenly knew I couldn't take it a second longer—any more of this strain and I'd flip, go stark raving. The hell with the last trunk—it had to be *now!* I sat in the pilot's seat, as if resting, my left hand slid under the seat, gripped the cold wrench.

"We want to avoid official attention, if possible. Do you have any company labels? We'll put them on the trunks. Your story is—we're making a routine flight for Pan-Texas. These are tool chests and I'm one of the company employees . . . Kelly, you listening? Have you any company labels, or tags?"

"Yes. I . . . I . . . think so," I mumbled and let go of the wrench. It was no go—I couldn't kill, not in cold blood. I *wasn't* Johnson—thank God!

He was staring up at me with that mocking grin again. He said softly, "Man, you're out on your feet."

I guess the 'man' touch did it, the final straw. Johnson and his lousy thoroughness, his damn smile! I heard myself say coldly, "Don't worry about me," and stepped out on the wingwalk, jumped down beside him.

The lantern jaw was a target I couldn't miss. I clipped him with a hard right, feeling the shock ride up to my shoulder. His blue eyes turned glassy as he fell backwards, out cold. Rubbing my numb knuckles for a moment, staring at the red bubbles of blood gushing from a corner of his slack mouth, I frisked him. The knife was strapped to his ankle. There wasn't much else in his pockets—the passport, about seventy bucks in USA money, lira, and a few francs. He looked almost comical, laying there in the wheat, a study in still life, his silly camera case still hanging from his neck—the sleeping tourist.

Okay, I couldn't kill him, but I'd take off with the two trunks, leave him the last one—let him take it from here as best he could. If he wanted to stalk me for the rest of my life—so be it. There wasn't anything else I could do.

All I needed now was time to take-off.

Johnson groaned. Taking a hunk of cable from the plane tool box I was about to tie his hands but changed my mind. I bound his ankles together, tied them to the handle of the last trunk—the one still on the ground. I knew the handle wouldn't hold long, but I couldn't leave him with his hands tied to die a slow death in the wheat—it might be weeks before anybody came. I had his knife and it would take him at least an hour to get his feet free—by then I'd be long gone.

As I put my foot on the retracting-in-flight step to the wingwalk, I heard him chuckle, turned to see him grinning at me with his bloody lips, the blue eyes actually a sneer. He said, "I knew you couldn't kill me, Kelly. You're greedy—but soft!"

I held up the Italian army knife. "And you'll never bury this in my back, Johnson, or whatever your real name is! Were you going to wait until we were airborne, then knife me, land some place in Germany?"

He tried to look puzzled, but it was far too late for acting. "What are you gassing about, man? I meant I knew you'd get greedy, try to take it all for yourself. Man, that's only nature with so much loot . . ."

"Cut the slang act. Although you damn near had me fooled. You and your Kraut thoroughness—memorizing a baseball record book, getting a phony passport with a simple name like James Johnson! I almost took the line, sinker

151

and all, but you made a couple of mistakes—big and little mistakes!"

"Kelly, are you out of your living mind? I've heard of treasure making guys go nuts, but. . . ."

"Come on, the show's over—you rang the curtain down on your act this morning. I admit I only thought it odd about you low-rating Willie Mays as a ball player because of his color. Even when you knifed your buddy, scar-face, double-crossing him without a word or a moment's hesitation, I didn't get the picture—of Nazi ruthlessness. I don't know what kind of a story he was supposed to slip me, but the two of you were going to do me in. Of course the big mistake, where you really struck out, you phony baseball buff, was telling me my Cessna could take off from the field. I never told you the kind of plane I flew, and only a pilot would know a twin engine Cessna can make it on a field of this length! I came awake then fast, old buddy, got the picture—the whole message, finally! Scar-puss was the SS man guarding Il Duce, you—the Luftwaffe pilot! Sure you knew exactly where the loot was, you two put it in the cave back in 1945!"

Baldy spit out a bloody pearl, still seemed to be mocking me with his cold eyes as he shook his head, told me, "Man, you need lots of sleep. A little rest and . . ."

"You're wasting time, just how dumb do you think one guy can be? You two jokers must have been in a hell of a stew all these years—a fortune waiting if you could figure a way of getting it out of Italy. You were so hard up, even tried propositioning the Italian government, but they turned you down. Your old Blackshirt pals would have helped with their gangs of dumb kids, but that would have meant slicing the pie far too many ways. Wanted the loot for yourselves, and in the long run—to take it alone. Needed a plane: a boat was no good because it would be too risky transporting the loot to the coast, and the Italian government would love tossing your can under the jail as a war criminal. Okay, either you could never raise enough money to buy a plane, or couldn't get the proper papers . . . and then you saw me, Kelly the pigeon!"

Johnson sat up—awkwardly—on his elbows. "Have you gone nuts, Kelly? You saw my USA passport."

"Sure. I'm taking it—Washington will be interested

152

in seeing it! My boss is sent to the hospital by a nut with a scar on his cheek in a dumb accident on an empty road. I'm attacked the same night—for no reason—giving you a chance to come to my rescue. Dropping the forged passport was a neat touch, the old American buddy-buddy role. You had a . . ."

"How the hell could I forge a passport, Kelly? Man, stop babbling like an idiot! If you're shaking me down for a larger cut, you have me over a barrel."

"Kraut, stop wasting time by running your dumb mouth! You thought you had a sucker in me, and a plane which wouldn't be searched by any authorities—Pan-Texas craft making a routine hop to Paris, or wherever you really had in mind to land. You had it all so carefully figured, my boss in the hospital, me with time on my hands. As you said, you even counted on my not being able to kill . . . a rat. Maybe I am soft . . . I can't kill you! Get this, I'm giving you a break—keep the last trunk, get out of the country with it any way you can. But I'm warning you, if I ever see your ugly puss again, I'll kill you!"

As I turned on the wingwalk, for the cabin, he said, "You'll never see me again, boy, or anybody else. You want it in the back or are you man enough to face death?" There was a terrible harshness to his voice. "Turn around slowly, if you can face me!"

I spun around to see his sweaty camera case open, a snub-nosed .38 in his hand, pointed up at me. I had a wild thought—he'd stepped out of character, should be holding a Luger. He said, "You're a boy trying to pull a man's job. No, don't move, Kelly! Not even going to make you untie me—you might get lucky. I'll do that when you're dead! You fool, the documents alone are worth a fortune in black . . ."

The bald dome of his head suddenly cracked open, exploded in dull red blood and soggy pink brain matter, splattering his monk's ring of blond hair—before I heard the small bark of a rifle.

CHAPTER 6

Hitting the ground so hard my head cleared, I felt around frantically, ran my hands up Johnson's legs and body . . . before I found the .38 wet with his blood and brains.

Huddled next to the dead man I was covered with icy sweat as I tried to decide whether I could make it into the plane, or crawl away in the wheat. It would take me minutes to start the Cessna's engines: I'd literally be a sitting duck for the rifleman, a. . . .

From not very far off in the darkness a woman's voice called out in English, "Kelly! Stand up with your hands over the head. We do not wish to harm you!"

Something about the throaty sound was familiar. I asked, "Who are you?"

"Marisa, *Signore* Kelly. Please stand up slowly—doll."

Shoving the gun into my boot I got to my feet, hands above my head, aware of the great target I made against the faint light from the plane door.

I heard steps coming toward me, then the light from a powerful flash walloped my eyes. Blinking furiously, turning my head aside, I saw Marisa walking through the wheat, holding the light. Everything was so absolutely unreal—she was wearing high-style tight black leather pants showing off fine legs, while a hooded pink sweatshirt framed her warm face. I had this feeling she was merely walking in from the beach at Viareggio—although there was hardly anything dreamy about the black automatic swinging from her neck by a leather strap, nestling between the wonderful hills her breasts formed in the sweatshirt. It was plain she wasn't wearing a bra.

There was a beefy man in his 50s on one side of her, a tall kid on the other side. The older man carried a powerful rifle in his thick arms—wore an old winter underwear top shoved into dark work pants. A pale blue scarf above a torn white skirt was knotted around the teenager's thin neck, and along with his heavy glasses it all added to an owlish look. But the hairy legs beneath the brown shorts had the good muscles of a soccer player. He sported a burp gun with a hell of a long shell clip. Both men stared at me with emotionless eyes.

Marisa smiled, the same flash of hot excitement I remembered so well. "Drop your hands, Mr. Kelly. But please, try nothing foolish. We think of you on our side, in this."

"I'm with you, Marisa, all the way!" I told her, cautiously lowering my mitts. The old man's thick finger seemed welded to his rifle trigger. "Sure quite a coincidence, you knowing about this, honey."

Marisa shook her pretty head. "Coincidence? Ah yes, I know what you mean. But no, we do not work so . . . so . . . how you say? . . . so careless. When neo-fascists attacked you that night in Viareggio, we must find out why. We even search your hotel room. But we get very interested when informer tell us this one—" Marisa pointed a blue-sneakered foot at Johnson—"arrange it all. Then, when you were so curious with me about Dongo treasure . . . we follow you all the time. You see, we try leave little to . . . chances."

"Yeah. I thought I saw you in Milan, had the feeling I was being tailed. Now what?"

"I like think you were doing this under—big stress, Mr. Kelly, but you always had in mind turn trunks over to our government."

"Sure, I guess so. You bet! I was ready to fly to Rome!"

"Yes, I think maybe that why the Nazi about to kill you. Well, we also want chests. We . . ."

"A four way split?" I asked, suddenly full of relief. "That's okay with me." I smiled at the two gunmen. Nothing changed in their faces.

"*Split?* Oh doll, you are wonderful!" Marisa said, looking lovely as she grinned up at me. "There should be very important documents in chests, proving who worked with

155

the Nazi swine in high offices and still remain in high places. *That* is what we seek."

"And the loot, the gold?"

"It will be put to best use, in time return to the real owners, the Italian people."

"Returned by you?"

"By my party. No one person shall gain, that is the truth."

I knew I'd been had—again. "What about him?" I asked, confused, nodding down at Johnson.

"We shall also put him to his best use—fertilizer for this field. I tell them to remove the other two trunks from your aircraft. All right, *Signore* Kelly . . . Kent?"

"Sure," I said, as if I had any choice.

She rattled off something in Italian. The older man nodded at me and Marisa must have told him not to worry. They had a grunting tough time getting the trunks out, but still it was easier than lifting them onto the plane. I told them to be damn careful of the wingwalk.

The old guy was strong as a cage of apes, he and the owl-faced young fellow actually *threw* the trunks out. I had this horror feeling they would land on Johnson, smash his corpse . . . and didn't know why that should worry me. The last trunk came flying through the faint cabin light, hit the trunk to which Johnson was still tied, happily bounced off on the other side. When it hit the ground, the top split open.

Marisa turned her flash on the loot. All I could think of was—it looked exactly like a burglar's swag. I expected rows of neat gold bars . . . but this was a jumble of papers, silver plate, gold cups, rings and diamond stickpins by the hundreds, plus old fashioned watches, spoons, even gold crosses. Instead of the treasure of a dictator it seemed more like the haul of a cat burglar who'd ransacked a villa.

The teenager bent down and excitedly thumbed through the papers, calling out names to Marisa. The older man poked at the rings with his heavy shoe. There was much fast Italian being traded back and forth, most of which I couldn't understand. But I was suddenly full of hope once more—the papers really seemed more important to them than the jewels.

Marisa's lush lips smiled at me. She asked, "Before you fly away, Kent, do you want some of this, as a reward?"

"No."

"As a souvenir?"

I shook my head. Both men were busy bending over the open trunk, the jewels sparkling like a sky-full of tiny stars in the light of the flash. "Marisa, listen to me!" I whispered quickly. "They want the papers, those documents —let 'em have 'em! I have a gun in my boot, can disarm them. With the jewels we can live the rest of our lives on some South Sea island! Honey, this is our chance for adventure and romance, for . . . !"

"Kent, can you not understand the importance of this? The papers will convict and expose mass murderers! My own brother died before a Nazi firing squad. My father was tortured by Mussolini's . . ."

I squeezed her shoulder. "Not so loud, honey. I'm all for the swine getting it, and the papers will do the trick. I'm talking about us, *you and me*. They get the evidence and we take enough to live happily on an island, our own little world of joy—we'll have it made!"

Her dark eyes seemed sad. "Kent, there are no 'little' worlds any more, or even big ones, which can not be reached. Italy is my country, why should I want to leave it, flee to some island?"

"Because you said you were a child of war—have adventure in your blood. Like me! Marisa, I could go for you and . . . you call me a living doll. Honey, it will be paradise. I'll even marry you . . ." The look of utter amazement on her pretty face made my words peter out.

"Kent, I call you doll because that is what you are, pretty and nice to see, but not yet awake up here." She tapped her hooded head. "Up there, you indeed like a doll. As for marrying you, I am flattered you ask, but I am married. The boy who helps me on the beach is Rinaldo, my son. My husband cooks the cakes and. . . ."

"The blind man?" I mumbled.

"Ay, he lost his eyes in the war, fighting fascism."

I didn't believe her. "I've never seen a ring on your left hand?"

She smiled. "I do not wear a wedding band because the salt air will harm it. I am most happy with my son, very in love with my fine husband. As you say in your slang, I already have it made—why should I seek an island, leave my dear ones?"

For a moment we merely stared at each other. I felt like the world's champion horse's rear. Marisa asked, "Doll, you are certain you do not want some of . . . jewels, for your trouble? For a souvenir?"

"I don't collect souvenirs, that's for suckers." My voice was barely a whisper.

"Then I think best you fly now. And Kent, it be no good for any of us to ever talk about this. In time it all may come out, maybe in the pages of history, but for now, you not speak of it, nor will we. You understand?"

I nodded.

She reached up, patted my cheek. "You are sweet, Kent. Other days, other times, we might have best fun on that island you think still possible to find—outside of cinema, or dreams."

I squeezed her hand. "Thanks for the brush-off, Marisa."

"I mean it, other times. . . ."

"Yeah. Don't give me a sisterly kiss—I'm too bushed to take that."

Her face looked puzzled. Then, pulling her hand from mine, she slowly patted my cheek again. "Also, please do not attempt use gun you have in your boot. Kent, when I was small girl I only have one doll, I never like break it." She touched the automatic hanging between her swaying breasts.

"I know, you used an empty hand grenade for a rattle." I pulled Johnson's .38 from my flying boot, handed it to her—butt first. "Add this to your charm necklace. Tell your friends to hold tight to their precious papers in the prop backwash. So long, Marisa."

Climbing into the Cessna I switched on the landing lights, started the twin engines roaring in the night. As I taxied down the field, wing-tip tanks seeming to float on a sea of wheat, turned for take-off. . . . I saw Marisa wave, blow a kiss at me.

Once airborne, I pulled up the landing gear, circled sharply to gain altitude. For a split second I saw them below in a tiny circle of light.

Looking at my dirty clothes, feeling my unshaved face,

I wondered if I'd scare hell out of Valerie, barging in on her before breakfast.

But Valerie would understand—probably understand too damn well. A long sleep plus lots of living, much talking and Valerie's cold, common sense—that's what I needed, and badly. Of course I'd never tell her about tonight, never really be able to tell anyone—perhaps in time I wouldn't believe it myself. But I *had* to be with Valerie *now*.

I knew I was being pushed into . . . something. That I'd lost . . . I didn't know exactly what. It was simple and it was confusing. I wanted only to see Valerie, was rushing to her at 240 mph. I was happy. I was also sad.

I gave up trying to figure things out, plotted a Paris course on my maps . . . well aware I was also flying directly to that split-level in Kew Gardens.

I not only felt exhausted . . . but very old.

— END —

Printed in the United States
By Bookmasters